SEXUAL BLOOD

SEXUAL BLOOD

a novel by
Mark Amerika

BLACK ICE
BOOKS

Published by Fiction Collective Two with support given by the
English Department Unit for Contemporary Literature of
Illinois State University, the English Department Publications
Center of the University of Colorado at Boulder, and the Illinois
Arts Council

Address all inquiries to: Fiction Collective Two, Unit for
Contemporary Literature, Campus Box 4241, Illinois State
University, Normal, IL 61790-4241

Sexual Blood
Mark Amerika

ISBN: Paper, 0-57366-000-0

Produced and printed in the United States of America

FOR FREE SPIRITS EVERYWHERE
AND NOWHERE

SEXUAL BLOOD

I. NUTRIENCE

II. PRACTICE

The Songs of Maldoror

III. THERAPY, OR THE REVOLUTION OF EVERYDAY LIFE

IV. ESCHATOLOGY

NUTRIENCE

The door of the womb always on the latch...
Deep in the blood the pull of paradise.
The Beyond. Always the beyond...
—Henry Miller

THE LAST THING HE WRITES IS THIS:

HE WOULD BECOME A TERRORIST: HE WOULD FUL-FILL HIS OWN DESIRES AND START RANDOMLY ASSERTING HIS CREATIVE SELF WHEREVER HE FELT LIKE IT: HE WOULD BECOME AN ARTIST: THE ONE OCCUPATION CURRENTLY UNDER SIEGE AS BEING MOST CRIMINAL IN ACTIVITY: HE WOULD TRANSPORT AN UNHINGED PRIMITIVE FLOW INTO THE UNDOMESTI-CATED WILDNESS OF HIS BODY SO AS TO DELIVER THE MOST FRENZIED STATE OF TRANSGRESSION EVER CREATED:

BUT: IN ORDER TO SET THIS RADICAL AGENDA IN MOTION: THE FIRST THING HE WOULD HAVE TO DO: WOULD BE: TO BECOME:

WOMAN

He had found himself unable to play anything for weeks.

This temporary inability to create himself out of nothing was all new to him. Previous to this experience was the inevitability of going to the digital-audio workstation every day and cranking out whatever his imagination felt was necessary. It could be anything from post-punk noise assemblage to funkadelic folk to anarchic grunge rock. The white flash of exploding consciousness losing sight of itself in acts of pure creation was what he most enjoyed out of life. He had always thought of it as a birthright. Why had he all of a sudden lost the instinctive blow-away energy that enabled him to engage himself in this necessary activity?

His most recent routine was to wake up, bypass the workstation, get dressed (haphazardly, no shower, no breakfast) and immediately head for the nature trails. Living up against the foothills of the Colorado Rockies provided him ample opportunities to get lost in the wilderness. Without even broaching the slightest clarity of consciousness, he would find himself rambling through the pine forest with nothing particular on his mind although eventually he'd get stuck in the formal possibilities of whatever new song he happened to be writing at the time and try to build on its potentiality. But since he was no longer capable of writing any new songs, the formal possibility he was presently caught in was of the how-to-get-back-to-work-without-really-trying variety. That was the way it had always been. Not Trying. Just Doing. Just being a player lost in the ecstasy of nonstop power-cranking.

After weeks of walking the forest and finding nothing that would help explain what he now saw as a working disorder, he decided he was finished. Kaput. Finito. End of story. Portrait of the Artist as a Dead Young Man. Period.

Then, one day, walking the usual route across the Shadow Canyon ridge heading West toward the Continental Divide, a restless spirit took hold of him. It was as if he were walking into yet another phase space he had no control over. He looked up and saw a perfect blue sky, but instead of synchronizing his anxious heart with its supposedly cloudless harmony, he wondered aloud to himself if this divine ceiling of life-protecting atmospheres were nothing but a fraudulent covering, a fashionable airlocked dome that hid the terrible black madness he knew he could easily transform himself into. He quite readily began dreaming of his eventual parlay into the hidden black space of the future he desperately wanted to become so as to finally get it all over with, and in losing himself inside this reckless dream of becoming nothing but the trajectory of a timeless speed zooming into the ever widening hole of absolute nothingness, he felt himself radically transforming his sense of personal identity. What was this strange attractor that kept enfolding his consciousness in upon itself?

He wasn't sure what this new operating mode of existence was or what it would have to offer by way of pleasure-filled experience, but at the moment it didn't matter. What mattered was that he felt himself casually walking into a new phase space, a heretofore unheard of formulation that distributed itself in a multiplicity of concurrent flows. A wave of momentum pushed him forward as he moved his way up and around the mountain. Everything inside him felt juiced to the max. The sensational vibration he felt himself becoming was bodywide. These hardcore electric pulsations were now turning him on to the ultimate power-trip of all, as if turning his head up and kissing the sky could put him into an unrealized Feedback Heaven.

His mind began mapping out a variety of possible routes to lose itself in. Without even thinking about it, he started chanting a trancelike mantra with imaginary guitars filtering through his brain. He sang:

> What are we gonna do after the orgy
> What are we gonna do after the pain
> What are we gonna do after the party
> What are we gonna do after the rage
>
> Commodify my heart
> Commodify my presence
> Commodify my art
> Commodify my absence
>
> It's morning in Amerika
> It's morning in Amerika
> It's morning in Amerika
> I'm mourning for Amerika
>
> God rest their souls
> Heaven is NOT a Superbowl

An ironic smile whipped across his face. He could finally see himself rocking again.

Maldoror came upon the Royal Arch.

Some few thousand years earlier, while glacial seas were gradually melting revealing rock protrusions that would eventually become the highest of Amerika's mountains, different stone fragments, their foundations slipping out from under them, met in mid-air collisions, some of them landing on the ground in perfect unison. This is what had happened here at what was now called Royal Arch. An inch or two in either direction and the two huge rocks would have immediately hit the ground becoming nothing but broken hearts gradually disintegrating into dust. But something had stopped them from free-falling and now, fused together for life, nose to nose, they stood bonded in holy matrimony till nuclear blast do they part. It was the epitome of an Earth in love with itself.

He stood before the great arch peering through its eroded openings out toward the clearest blue sky he could ever remember seeing. The clearheaded blue was phasing his mind into new acceptance. He sensed that the End Was Nearing but was unsure as to what exactly was Ending. Was it his life? It didn't matter. He envied the dust. Maybe, and he hoped it was true, it was the end of his suffering, of his inability to continuously become overly engrossed in the textual flow of energy he had so easily lost himself in many times before.

"*Please*," he yelled to some unforeseen Goddess of Fertility, "please make me make myself all over again. I *need* to create…I need to experience *pleasure*…."

As he yelled this, he had closed his eyes extremely tight, witnessing nothing except the red phosphorescence that his mind's eye created for him. He held onto that mesmerizing red spillover for as long as his eyes could take it, then let go, opening up the visual portholes to whatever effect of beauty the world had to offer him.

As if he had created it himself, a barely perceptible trail found its way up the mountain just to the northwest of where he was standing. He had been to the arch a number of times before but had never noticed this trail. The thought of "have I really just envisioned this trail into being" came across his mind. He would never catch himself thinking "all the other times I've been up here I've just blinded myself to the other possible routes that lead to discovery, perhaps on *purpose*, so as to not get too far off track." For a moment, it felt as though too many disparate thoughts were filling his head. How the trail got there and why he had never seen it before became irrelevant. He was rapidly becoming whatever he needed to become and it didn't matter *what* he believed. All he knew was that he felt it was time to break the static mold that everybody else seemed so eager to become.

Not wanting to pay attention to the many thoughts that were trying to displace his flow, he conquered the nastiness of their confusing presence by running up this trail. He didn't care where it led to. He didn't worry about the time or what errands he might have to run back in town. The stress of all the world's conflicting viewpoints and all the superficial hype that went along with them was quickly melting away. He just ran. Fluid petrified fabulous running.

About thirty minutes and one incredible aerobic workout later, he came upon another apparition of seemingly worn trail and decided to take that too.

Within ten minutes he was at a thin oval-shaped cave. A green and yellow and red tapestry of lichen surrounded the cave entrance. From where he stood it look like an enlarged vagina with technicolor pubic hair. He thought he smelled

13

the dank erotica of a woman just come. Closing his eyes and breathing in deeply, he felt an uncontrollable urge to masturbate out in the open air. A rush of blood funnelled straight to his cock and he pulled it out softly taking hold of it and slowly jerking the entire shaft imagining that all of Nature's open space was his to jizz in....

Maldoror had wanted to become a Woman. He was sure that this was the way to infiltrate the Powers That Be, an infiltrate he felt was necessary so as to be able to destabilize their hierarchy of Death. Once a Woman, he thought, I can turn the world on its head. I must seek the necessary means that will lead me to an appropriate Internal Transformation, then begin the social endeavor I've been put on this planet for.

He felt sure that the only way to eventuate this possibility of activating change in the world was to develop both a supersonic love energy and a means of deploying it. A love energy that would fill the Earth's crust in such a way that it would vibrate into the living bones of all people caught in the great gravitational pull.

Wild thoughts were growing in the far reaches of his mind. Lush idealism pulling at the roots of his being. Feeling *alive*.

"This planet," he thought to himself, "this planet is dreary. And yet, despite all sci-fi explorations into the Great Beyond, life does not exist elsewhere and Man is still relegated to earthly residence. There *is* no science-fiction. It just doesn't exist. *This* exists. This cave."

Standing before the cave, these thoughts streaming through his totally adulterated mind, he wished he had some drugs. Or a beautiful woman. Or the ability to think through his sexuality.

He didn't want a sex-change operation. He wasn't really interested in hormone shots. He didn't want synthetically-altered skin-graft genitals. He wasn't interested in gender therapy (his consciousness constantly fed him opportunities to become whatever he wanted). All he knew was that the Phallic Symbol he was born with was really perfect for penetration and that penetration wasn't so much a bad thing as it was a necessary practice. It was the opposite of being morose. It was the opposite of taking. It was his chance to share himself as a vehicle of Pleasure. Now if only he could become a *Herself* capable of penetrating those certain select Others who were constantly presenting themselves to him, then maybe that would be a start. A beginning. A way to change the world.

To each being, several other lives were due. The psychic conflagration of thought burning up inside him was telling him that it was first necessary to become a Woman before he could even begin to have any effect on the rapidly degrading society on Earth they now called Amerika.

All of this was smoothly asserting itself into his cheese-mold brain as he tried to focus on the deliverance of the cave before him. No burning bushes, he thought. No voice of God. Just an opening. An entryway into the mouth of portal causality.

Inside the cave, on a bed of pine needles, slept the Medicine Woman. Her sensitivity to the rapidly changing Presence now manifesting itself in her secluded environment caused her to stir. She blinked an eye open. Seeing Maldoror was Seeing The Future.

"Seeping Vision," she quietly whispered and forced herself up and into the lotus position.

"Please," she said to the towering Mal, "sit here with me. I want to feel your Presence. I want to take you in."

"I already know what you're here for," she told Mal. "I have been dreaming your escape up here. Your entire route has traced the paths of my most recent dreams. Feel."

She took Mal's hand and put it on her moist love jungle.

"All the animal kingdom lives in here," she said. "Lions and Tigers and Bears. The only animal that I refuse to let live inside here is corrupt Man."

"But…" Maldoror was going to ask her a question but she had already anticipated it in her dream.

"…yes, you want to know about Woman. Woman is not corrupt Man. Man is the final ooze of demon leakage."

Maldoror wasn't sure he exactly knew what she was talking about.

"You will," said the Medicine Woman. "Demon leakage infects your imaginary universe even as you desperately try to finally unfinish yourself in acts of random songwriting. It is your mortal enemy, one that you will continually encounter as you set yourself on that Journey toward the Unknown we, out of convenience, call Chaos. Are you ready?"

Things were moving very fast. The quick-draw dialogue of the Medicine Woman was putting him in an awkward state of mind. He felt an uncontrollable rush of adrenalin take him over as he tried to process her high-energy philosophical spell. AT THAT VERY INSTANT he was also consciously trying to maintain a kind of equilibrium that would enable him to make sense of what he was experiencing. He recognized the danger of the ensuing confusion as Losing Sight of Himself. He knew he was Losing Sight of Himself because the more he felt his self slipping away into the control of the Other, the surer he was of the necessity of this takeover experience actually happening. He thought to himself: The Slow Slide Into Pleasure displaces the human element and

17

foregrounds the Imagination Itself. No control. Just the creative energy of the moment transgressing the manmade laws of Desire. And I don't even *know* her.

"Ready for what?" asked Mal, courteously, yet still confused.

"To take the drug," was all she said, deadpan, a done deal.

"Okay," he said, opening himself up to whatever happened next. This was his to lose or so he thought (kaleidoscopic fragments of self disappearing in the process).

The Medicine Woman explained that the psycho-pharmakinetic effect of acidophilus mixed with a special legume grown near the Aztec ruins in the Yucatan would provide him with the necessary proactive stimulant one needs in order to transform Internal Gender Identity (IGI). She said that the Mexican bean was responsible for activating the latent Sexual Blood (she used the term Sexual Blood as if it were a way of life). This activation caused a mirrored aphrodisiac effect. Instead of producing in the person who took the drug an incredible urge to screw anything that had a genital attached to it, the intaker of said drug would emit an aura of irresistible libidinal energy that would make *certain select Others* mad with the prospect of screwing *It*. *It* was the sexual creature that, in spite of or in consolation with the body it had been given, took the drug. Not everybody would be attracted to the sexual It. Only certain select Others would be unabashedly magnetized to the sexual It. These certain select Others were filled with Unforeseen Need. Unforeseen Need was a chemical response to the aura emitted by the one who consciously carried and craved transmission of the Sexual Blood. This Unforeseen Need gave the Other an opportunity to become the It itself. The It itself, she explained, was the Sexual Blood. There was no way to know who the certain select Others were until one took the drug oneself. Once one took the drug and started encountering Others who were interested in becoming It by physically loving It, then one was allowed to share the secret of Sexual Blood with this Needy Other.

It should be noted, the Medicine Woman added, that just because one feels the need to *become* the Sexual Blood, they aren't automatically in a position to turn Others on *to* It. Becoming a Giver of Sexual Blood is something one has to successfully VISUALIZE by losing oneself in a terribly difficult Journey Toward Chaos. Which isn't to say that the Sexual Blood discriminates. Rather, Sexual Blood is blind to all stereotypes. It's just that one must really have the *spiritual capacity* to become this special altruistic donor of the live-vibe fluid. This fluid is a kind of extraterrestrial junk that gets shot into the bodies of those who have the Power to VISUALIZE It. Get It?

Maldoror stared in awe at the Medicine Woman. Did he get it? He heard her say "How often?" but the joke passed him by. All he could conjure up inside his degenerative brain was that yes, he *was* getting something. But what was it? Fortunately (or maybe it was unfortunately) his body wouldn't let him try to figure it out.

He could feel his entire skeleton turn into a kind of malleable taffy. The Absolute Need to *become* the Sexual Blood was causing him to VISUALIZE himself tightly wrapped around the living coat of flesh that was speaking to him. He felt unabashedly magnetized to the bright red aura of the Medicine Woman as it permeated his sensitive bodyspace.

The Medicine Woman called the drug *Acid Pornosophilus*. "Ingesting Acid Porn is the necessary first step one takes in preparing for IGI Transformation," she explained to him.

19

"The process of gradual internalization that slowly takes place within your battered psyche will enable you to become a Freeform Feminine Construct yet will only strengthen your outer Male Category. Others will view you as typical white male patriarchal scum. You'll wonder why you constantly experience a feeling of genderlessness. You won't want to see yourself as one *or* the other. Which is fine. Gender creates ideology. Ideology disrupts the meta-flow of collective consciousness' creative intensity. So your mission, should you decide to accept it, would be to use your hard body to infiltrate the susceptible Hierarchies of Death created by Goon Men and their squads of Passive Doers. You see," the Medicine Woman looked at Maldoror's eyes for the first time and he noticed, immediately realized beyond doubt, that her eyes were the same flaming green cat eyes that he himself had been given at birth, "Power, and I mean capital P, resides in the innermost parts of Feminine Being. It has been appropriated in the most violent of ways by Goon Men. But what they have acquired is not so much the *essence* of Power, rather, they have assimilated its empty, overprocessed, inertiated form. The power, and I mean little p, they have managed to accumulate over the last few thousand years, is as empty as a Twinkie. It has the total sum nutrient of one M&M candy. The Feminine Being Power that I'm going to turn you on to is going to blow your mind. You will be able to live on this line of activity for as long you feel your Creative Presence is needed. You may wish to call this road I'm taking you on Nutrience. There are many reasons why we might want to call it this but I believe it's better for you, during your Journey, to extricate whatever meaning and/or personal significance (and it *is* personal!) there might be there for you *yourself*. For now, I will ask you to go into the Tripping

Chamber where you'll find a space filled with nothing but your own ability to Imagine what it is you need to become. Your bliss is waiting for you somewhere here on Earth. Existence is fragile and to imagine other worlds isn't really good practice. Ground yourself in the Paradise of HERE. Work with what you've got NOW: the hypothetical Earth of today. Use your mind to VISUALIZE the New You, or maybe I should say the Next You, the amalgamated fictional construct of choice. You're totally capable of doing this Mal. Totally. And remember: Fiction is the Instinctive Desire To Interpolate Arbitrary Pseudo-Autobiographical Experiences Into Collective History's Dialogue With Itself or, if you prefer, Hyperreal Application of Specially Selected Samples of Processed Text That **YOU YOURSELF** Have Appropriated In Order To Generate **Your Own** Current Operational Mode of Being: I'm talking about your Imagination, Mal, the creative apparatus that proactively engages you with the Force of Nature. That Force is what we call Nutrience. It's your Sexual Blood.

"You will inevitably find *your own* Imagination strong enough to work out the political implications of the societal prison your mortality imbeds you in. That's a reality even breathing scientists have to deal with. Every human's gonna die, right? Meanwhile, you, dearest Maldoror, will find your bliss here on this Earth and it will entitle you to tireless attempts at turning Others on to theirs. All you have to do is remain diligent in taking this drug and the ensuing effects will assist you in fortifying enough feminine energy within your hard body to accommodate the forthcoming feelings of gender confusion which will seem more like genderlessness. But I'm already digressing more than you're prepared for," she said, and Maldoror was quickly becoming aware of his

21

unconditional love for the spacy Soul Woman whose shamanistic tendencies were already having their desired effect on him.

"Take this with you," she smiled at him. It was a capsule the color of a kidney bean. It was Acid Porn.

The Tripping Chamber was in the far reaches of the cave. Hanging love beads seperated him from the room where the Medicine Woman had been sleeping. A half dozen lit candles gave the space an eerie feel. There was the smell of exotic incense. The floor was swept clean and had a small Persian-styled rug on it. The rug was mostly red with a gold, black and white pattern shaped like an eagle's head.

Maldoror sat on the rug in the lotus position. His intestines twisted and a bubble of gas displaced itself coming out as a loud long fart the odor of which reached his nostrils immediately. It was a life-affirming smell that reminded him of his dead father who could never understand Mal's desire to become a rock musician.

He had trouble swallowing the capsule. He couldn't dream up enough spit to help slide it down. "Damn, it's always the simple things."

Then he started VISUALIZING the Medicine Woman. She was still in her tattered sundress. White with tiny blue wildflowers enmeshed in the fabric. Barefoot and her long curly blond-gray hair flowing behind her back, down in front of her shoulders, everywhere. Only now, sitting alone in the Tripping Chamber, could he even begin to VISUALIZE what the Medicine Woman looked like. He *never* paid attention to detail. Especially while being spoken to. Her voice. What was it about her voice that made him feel elastic? He could stretch himself all around her. A human snake with flagellating skinhairs flicking its way across her sumptuous body. Strange attractor.

Eyes dripping seeping demon leakage. Meaning flawed. Annulled hyperactivity of supposed being. Salivates.

Words gurgling. Mouthwash of desire. Wanting to VISUALIZE. Become the Sexual Blood. Her.

Mal swallows.

Mellow mallow cups of milky motherhood drape him in liquid dementia. The Hypnotic Hues of Heavenly Herness spreads its perfectly sphinctered layers of inner leg muscle and straddles his face. Immateriality delivers estranged configurations of death love disaster pleasure boring head sinking into the treasure grove of ultimate wet pleasure.

Perfumed pubis uno eternal umberto slave lover latin lover makeshift tongue squeezing rolled playdough flesh. Fresh imprint of madagascar eye shadow dripping down her face in random cartographic survival zones. Fragrant french kiss deep sucking him in so hard he almost. Present tense reaches catastrophic breaking point. Only Her. Hypnotic. Sexual Blood. Leaking.

Galaxy gridlocks. Sends sense sidereally. Torrential downpour of womanly cum cremates early morning cluster. She's not saying anything she's not saying anything she's not saying anything but body writhing and sounds lost in moonhowl foregoing decodification translation comprehensibility. Prehensile claws erupt. Strumming clit on teethy strings eating flesh guitars while electric white ladyland succumbs. The long drawn-out moans of heavenly feedback filling the bowels of the cranky universe junked on dirty love....

Mal can no longer think. He

eats
sucks
devours

24

sucks
devours
sucks

heads into the marrow of cuntrock that presses up against him.

He cannot stop being Me.

Me is for Mortals.

Mortal morsels stuck between the teeth.

All *dente.*

All deterioration.

Mal's hallucinating apparatus gets locked over a short transcription of words that float in his screenlike mind bending in waves of uncertainty. He sees

Come   Alive

    Freak   Meat

Come   Alive

    Freak   Meat

The smell of discharging cunt oil lubricates his disjointed armory of knee-jerk mouthing.

His eyes are wide open pupils dilated black holes freaking. Saucers. Flying out of his face into the abstract world of Ungodly Creation. An alien alienated from alienation. Thrice removed. *The ideal narcosis*. Mobilized fetal habitat. Embodying a cure. Himself: The Hyper-Herness Coming. Herness cumming dead white chickens beside the blazing rainwater. Burning red aura of hypnotic vibrations continually discharging.

A thought crosses his mind: it repeats itself over and over and over again and again and again until it's the only trip he's on: This Medicine Woman is him. He's Her. It's *his* pussy that suffocates him now as he tries to swallow the roasted cunt oil that trickles out of the weeping cuntrock. Sexual lunacy of visionary blood. *Cum gun red rum. Rhumbus mumble. Hump funt rumble. Grumble grumble. Grum.*

Grug. Grug grug grug. Gato gato grub grub. Grub.

(Hungry cat eating his pussy for dinner?)

Num. Nuh. Nuh nuh nuh nuh nuh nuh. Nug.

(Wanting now to automatically unwrite himself. To decreate that part of himself that aligns his pleasure enterprise with the programmatic plug-away poetry of guns and butter. To reinvestigate a potential writing of the body presently navigating its way through an uncharted space of nugs and tubers.)

Tumor nugs growing wild. Elastic limbs wrapping around each other while Internal Oblivion makes underground fiber-optic connexions. Satellite Love caught in a pearl jam rewired for optimum telegnosis.

Soul Brother drowning in the cauldron of thick black ink. No time to think. Eyes on the blink. On the brink...

Nug.

lost in the deepest darksleep his consciousness has ever drowned in, a feeling of contentment and the surety of being able to soon release himself in the white hot flash of chemical decomposition that he loves to lose himself in.

but at that point of total loss who can even call themselves a him. this is the question that haunts her. the her inside him. the her at the end of together. the thing he needs to be.

unable to approach her without wanting to be her he inevitably seeks to enter her. by entering her he becomes her. although her is not necessarily a category that easily recognizes itself either. nor is either. nor is or.

My

Art

Lay

Dead

On

Roads

Of

Ruin

RESET: FLANGE

The dichotomous regions his ancestors explored and conquered and ruined are no longer liveable. These lands that produced such grainy blurry sight unseen concepts as good and evil are now chemically obliterated. The only untapped terrain Mal can venture forth on is the neutral loam festering inside his brain. Nomad on the loose he travels into the depths of possibility. Here in the heart of his brain pumping bloodless eyes with the most advanced polyphasic electrical flows ever invented Mal hears his reconstructed soul-apparatus singe with the heat of the moment. The smell that reaches his nostrils is that of Internal Oblivion.

This Internal Oblivion is a high-voltage high-frequency high-potential alternate-current of libidinal energy that streams through his forlorn body discharging millions of micro-egos haphazardly searching for some form of comforting affection. With no affection in sight, he feels the rush of this herded pack of micro-egos destabilize his chemical balance. The present moment is highlighted by a light-intense heat flickering inside his brain, a burning strobelight of confusion that seems at once aimless and pursuant of some utopian future that can't possibly exist. Eventually the Internal Oblivion reroutes itself to both of his retinas where it then flows through his optic nerves which redistribute the druglike power of his seedy vision out into the phenomenological world that constantly disrupts his sense of becoming the ultimate form of unconscious desire he feels he needs to be.

Welcome To Tuber City!

The synthetic bomb culture food preservative culture slave labor culture has caused Mal to hallucinate a forever picnic. On his forever picnic he brings the thought of deflowering youth. Reflowering his anxious libido. Anything to reactivate the dormant grunge mechanism hiding inside his instinctive gut.

He envisions the forever picnic as if it already happened. As if he's already lived it and now only revises its impact on him. As if measuring the effect his dreams have had on his cultural environment were a way of seeing the future. As if it were happening now. In the past-present. Or a future-present where what one becomes rarely gets seen. Seen as in opened. As in opening one's culturally manipulated environment to the substance of one's raw dreams which can EXPLODE upon impact. Which is why he consciously explores the possibility of playing it out here in the flesh. HE JUST MIGHT EXPLODE. EXPLODE in the VISUALIZATION of his performance losing itself in process. Losing itself in the presence of something becoming the end of NOW.

The first thing he VISUALIZES is putting himself in proximity to young women. Fifteen sixteen maybe older. His gut response to their openended freeform vibe is to turn on to them. So he doesn't think about the ramifications he just turns on. By turning on to them he exposes himself to the underlying hate these young women have toward the authoritarian system of male patriarchy that decides in advance of their inevitable birth what they're supposed to do with themselves while living here on earth. And yet it's only after having successfully *turned on to them* that the young women share their radical secrets and dreams of empower-

SEXUAL BLOOD

ment with him. They can look into his eyes and see that he is one of them and that he is ready to unite and enrage.

When these young, experimental rave chicks look in his eyes they sense a present where what one becomes rarely gets seen or opened. He sees them and thinks one thing: TO OPEN.

He refers to the growing fury of these young women and their desire to use it in subtle acts of terrorist sabotage as the Vendetta Moondata. He comes up with the term when he meets a hip high school chick whose name is actually Vendetta Moondata. Her friends call her Moon. So he calls her Moon too because it's her friends who introduce him to her. You see, Maldoror is one of them. Or at least he can *become* one of them. It's one of his special features. He's ageless. It's a very weird kind of dorian gray thing he has going for him. The difference being that he can be any age he wants. Which means he can be young old middle-aged whatever. And he can act on any level of maturity he wants. This is the spell the Medicine Woman puts on him. This is after he and the Medicine Woman become partners. Limited sexual agreement where he agrees to suck pussy if she'll provide details of metaphysical existence and turn him on to herb mania wisdom. It's actually a pretty good deal. Especially for Mal the raging young artist whose portrait is always changing thanks to his dorian gray agelessness. If it wasn't for that he'd probably be dead by now. But he's not dead at all. He's a Come Alive Freak Meat motorhead who revs the restless libido in certain select Others who as Others come to him in the most ordinary circumstances. Like Vendetta Moondata. He went to the community swimming pool to do laps. It was supposed to be Adults Only. Anybody under eighteen was asked to not swim during this period. So Mal

31

became a 21 year-old local musician and got in the pool started doing laps. He was splendid in the water. He always did the breast-stroke strictly because he liked the sound and feel of it. Breast-stroke. He was breast-stroking when four teenage girls came to the side of the pool and watched. They giggled. They pointed. They whispered. They giggled again. Mal got self-conscious and came out of the pool only to notice three of the teeny-boppers as library groupies. Library groupies were young girls who hung out at the city's main library looking at material. Any material. Magazines books maps the young male librarians. That was Mal. He was a young male librarian. As a young male librarian he was about 32 years-old. 32 was comfortable because it got attention both ways. Young and old. So one of the teenies said *hey, did you get the new* People *in?* Mal was confused because he was playing a 21 year-old musician-swimmer but then he realized he was also a 32-year old librarian and remembered that these teenies always read the new *People* magazine whenever it came in. Vendetta Moondata was the only one he didn't recognize. She said something like I *hate People* and Mal fell in love. He was totally awestruck by the aura emanating from her thong-bikinied body. He immediately asked her who she was. She told him she was Vendetta Moondata. He clumsily asked her out for an ice cream. She got this big smile on her face showing off her thick sexy lips. The other girls went ohhhh but had to let it go. They weren't invited.

"But what does this have to do with the forever picnic?"

Well, the idea of a forever picnic peaked when he met Moon. It was all a part of this need Mal had to visually inhabit the thing he needed to become: the ideal feminine construct. She was dark-skinned and looked oriental. Darker than an American Indian but not coal-black African-American. She said she came from Dharmagone. She wouldn't say where Dharmagone was but it did sound pretty far away so Mal assumed she was very different. And all he could think about was dipping into her pool of unfiltered mudhoney, the sticky-sweet sap of her timeless body, the skinflick drug that would allow him to experience the ultimate in human nirvana.

"I want to go on a forever picnic," she said to Mal who had just bought her ice cream. She said these strange things like she was using Mal's battered up broken language but rephrasing it to suit her own Dharmagone orientation. There was an eerie telepathic quality about her. Something remote yet controlled.

"What's a forever picnic?" asked Mal.

"I don't know. I never really thought about it."

"Well I'm sure you can improvise something..."

"Sure, I can improvise anything. A forever picnic is when you take a blanket statement and spread it on the historical grass so that all the little ants can come up and eat everything you've brought with you. They go nuts over whatever crumbs you leave them. It's like trickle-down economics except there's no money involved. Just rhetoric. Ideology. Food for thought. Or maybe it's thought for food."

"Ideas."

"Well, yeah, but I'm talking about empty ideas. Manipulation. Propaganda. The opposite of Nutrience. More emphasis on synthetico-chemical matter than, say, natural things you create on the spot like feelings. Feelings are the organic compost of emotions one experiences over the years so as to help offset the brutal tensions one inevitably becomes overexposed to in synthetic culture. They're nurturing things that if you use in powerful and positive ways will

33

change the quality of the ants' lives forever."

"For better or worse till death do they part. Give me an example."

"Okay. You lay out this blanket statement about how everything your country does it does for freedom and democracy. You say that your country is the most powerful humane obedient soulful nation on earth and that anybody who's anybody always already knows this. You must always say *always already* so that the ants see your idea as definitively philosophical."

"Wait a second. I'm confused."

"What confuses you?"

"A couple of things. First of all, you sound like a derelict hybrid of Popular President and Post-Structuralist Philosopher. Throw in a little new-age flakiness and you got what? The truth? A grass-roots campaign to do away with the system's congenital corruption? I don't believe something like that can exist. We're *always already* bought out. Liquified. Ransacked. Obstructed.

"Cancer is a way of life, Moon, and contamination is the spiritual glue that keeps our polyvalent Amerikan souls together. Besides, you're an adolescent and adolescents don't *do* philosophy. They watch TV."

"Not when they're me. I'm different. Can I continue?"

"Yes, sure, go ahead, but remember, I'm not buying it."

"Yes, right, like you say, you're *always already* bought out. But that's okay. That's what motivates you. But let's get back to the basics: the forever picnic. Where does it take place? Don't answer. I'll tell you where: it takes place on that screen of mind that used to be your brain but is no longer a brain."

"What is it?"

"A receptacle. A receptacle of the spectacle which, as you

34

know, is being produced for your so-called enjoyment right now. This very instant the world is being created and interpreted for you. Turn on the TV and see for yourself. You don't even have to think anymore. Thinking's dead and gone just like dreaming is alive and well and selling itself to you right this very minute so buy it while it lasts! $14.95 for the exquisite dreaming! I know you Mal. You say you're not buying into it but look at your account. You're heavily indebted to those who help you dream."

"Dreams that money can buy…"

"That's right. It's your Native Amerikan birthright. Your fifth-generation surrealist manifesto."

"Okay, so I don't think. You'll do the thinking for me."

"We'll do the blinking for you too. You'll love it."

"Wait a second. Who's we?"

"We are the ones who want to go on the forever picnic. All of us. It's not like it's something alien being forced on everyone. This isn't science-fiction. This is something so real that it seems absolutely connected to ground-reality."

"How connected?"

"Connected enough for me to know that this Swiss Almond Vanilla ice cream tastes pretty damn good to me right now. I'm a Häagen-Dazs freak."

"But that's just information originating in your taste buds and being translated by your brain, which, according to you, isn't a brain anymore. Just a receptacle, right?"

"Yes, a receptacle. Your mind has become Eliot's Wasteland. A landfill. Culture de sac."

"But I thought I was *on* the road. Not at some self-imposed dead end. You know, beat personality lost on a Journey to Chaos."

"Uh-uh, sweety, *end* of the road. Barely breathing soon-to-be aborted project. *Always already*. Although it's true about the Journey to Chaos. You're on it right now. Being with me proves it. You just gotta plow through that rhetorical bullshit that constantly stands in your way. In fact there's a secret underground passage I know of that will lead you to yet another phase of this world that will assist you in your search for change. This phase is potentially detrimental to your well-being because if you can't cut it then you die. Instamatically."

"Instamatically?"

"Yes, the Supreme Vindication Of Life takes a quick snapshot of you and that's it. You're gone."

"Who gets the picture?"

"Well, it never gets developed. That's what's so sad about it."

"Isn't there even a negative to work off of?"

"Yes, but the Supreme Vindication of Life keeps it locked away in a memory vault. For its eyes only. Sorry, but that's the nature of the game."

"I don't believe it."

"You don't *have* to believe it. We'll do your believing for you too. All you have to do is slave-wage work."

"Sounds pretty miserable."

"It *is* miserable. That's why you have to escape. I'm telling you this for your own good."

"You sound like my mother, may she rest in peace."

"Nobody rests in peace. More wars *there* than you ever imagined."

"Okay, so heaven too is nothing but spectacle. But tell me something Moon. Besides being precocious, what makes you know everything?"

"I'm *there* baby. I've got the prime Nutrience: Sexual Blood."

"You too?"

"Yeah, me too. I can help you. There's a place where you can learn how to blow this shit away. I know how to get there."

"Where is it?"

"Well, we have to go back to my cave or I won't be able to transport you."

"A cave. Another cave. Sometimes it seems as though I spend my whole life in caves."

"Is that so bad?"

"No, I guess not. So you've heard of Nutrience, I noticed you mentioned it a few times…"

"Nutrience is the road you're on. Development of the Sexual Blood. Journey to Chaos. It leads to Nowhere but at least you're getting an idea of how to get there. Nowhere is where it all happens. It's Everywhere. I know. I know where. Repeat after me: I know where."

"I know where."

"I no/where."

"I no/where."

"I need be."

"I need be."

"I know where."

"I know where."

"I've been there."

"I've been there."

"I go there."

"I go there."

"I am there."

"I am there."

"I nowhere."

"I nowhere."

"It's that simple Mal. Push pull push pull. You're going to like it where I'm taking you. It's the most important stop along the way."

"What's it called? Where are you taking me?"

"I'm taking you home, to my home, Dharmagone."

"Let's do it."

"Okay. You got an ice cream moustache under your nose."

DHARMAGONE

On the way up the mountain to Moon's cave Mal tells her that he is many things at once: a) bored lonely kid: b) experimental adolescent sex monster: c) yuppie scumbucket overflowing with the need to transgress greed (hyperinflated sense of self): d) aging peacemonger: e) semi-retired gigolo: f) dying WRITERMAN: g) newborn newspeak whose flesh has dematerialized into postindustrial babble: gish.

Mal will tell stories over and over again and again but he will dislike himself immensely for having done so: he senses his own knee-jerk moralism creeping into his telling: he thinks knee-jerk moralism suggests the potential for progress and narrative is pseudo-progressivity with an emphasis on knee-jerk morality: he would rather see his life project explore the possibilities of hyperspace and timelessness: complete immersion in the

> silent buzz of THE PROCESS.
> subtle biz of THE PROCESS.
> suffering blues of THE PROCESS.
> singing blaze of THE PROCESS.

Mal looks in Moon's green eyes and sees the same shining path toward brilliance that the Medicine Woman flashed when he hung out with her:

"You mean…"

"Yes, I'm Everywhere. Ageless. Fecund. Seeping."

At this point in the trip Mal keeps flashing back to the original incarnation of the Medicine Woman whose voice still says things to him. This time it says: "Love thrives on the moon data. Silver glow grows wild in feminine imagination. More freak more youth. Tender buttons. Push pull push pull. Outstretch your prison canvas…."

Mal asks: "Why is it that I feel numb whenever I'm around you?"

"Because your existence sucks. There's no motivation to continue drooling over the mechanization of your environment. All it does is suck the energy out of your tired-ass self. You feel beyond fatigued and can't incorporate lovemaking into your life because time is money and money is the material that fuels your amerikan capitalist being."

"But I've fucked many times before."

"Sure, you've fucked more than your fair share of Barbie dolls whose daddies have made it possible for them to survive by being creeps who steal from the poor while lining the pockets of the rich. They take care of those that take care of them."

"Goon men take care of goon men."

"Yes, and goon women. Goon women are the ones that tell the goon men that what they're doing is wonderful. Brilliant. Heroic. Stratospheric."

"And yet the goon women are women, I mean, I thought the Imagination, being feminine, fueled by Sexual Blood, driven through the poetic apparatus that is flesh turning into

40

white hot flashes of chemical decomposition distorting itself to the point of unrecognizable waves of ultra-crispy turn-on energy…"

"Listen to me," said Moon (she was now metamorphosizing into a living reincarnation of the Medicine Woman), "you came to the caves to begin your Journey to Chaos. The only way you'll ever begin to change is if and when you can stop the world and see what it is you're in the process of becoming. It's that simple. 'We'll do your thinking for you. We'll do your blinking for you. We'll do your dying for you.' Do you really believe they're looking out for *you*? Are their interests the same as *yours*? Who are *they*? How are *they* really *you*? Are we all selfsame analogous beings being digitally remixed into that Great Supercomputer In The Sky? Is *your* transfluctuating momentum of love-sex energy anchored in the nationalist tendency of the country you live in? Who do you think *you* are?"

"Well, I'm Maldoror. I think. Or else some phoney construct that has absorbed all the lies. And if that is the case, then how do I rid myself of these phoney creatures that live inside me?"

"You become the Sexual Blood. It's process, baby, process. You think that just because you came up and did some Acid Porn that the whole world's gonna bend over for you. The world of man is deceiving you. I don't want to hurt you but I will do whatever it takes to turn you back into animal spirit. We'll give you the next powerful dose of Acid Porn soon. But first you must dismantle yourself. You're going to live in Dharamagone. For the time being I'm the only thing that exists and if you want to stop and see what it is you're in the process of becoming then you'll have to stop and see it in *me* first."

"But…"

"No buts. You said you wanted to write your songs again. You were dying with the inability to express yourself despite the fact that things inside you were begging for release. This is a sign of your illness. Fear. Guilt. Wanting. Not being able to become…"

"…Woman…"

"Yes, but it's not that easy. The first thing we'll do is we'll have you write your songs. I want you to write them all out of you. Just like the song you created on your way up here. It doesn't have to mean anything. It doesn't have to be created for an audience least of all me. The idea is to fortify your Imagination with Practice. What do you think VISUAL-IZATION is? Listen Mal: the continual release of your animal spirit in whatever language you find necessary is what you must contend yourself with. The idea is to write yourself as you are now into oblivion. Every artist has their own abstract way of functioning and yours will be just as different as anybody else's. The end product, whether it's words on a page, high-decibel feedback coming out of a boogie amp, pixels on a screen, whatever, doesn't matter. What matters is you watch it go. Watching it go is preparing yourself for the Truth. You can get at it, I know you can get at it. I'm going to open myself up to you. I want you to crawl inside me and enter the secret city of Dharmagone. When you emerge you'll have written down your chants and that will have been the end of you as you are now. Then we'll go from there. But for now, come. Come inside me. Crawl up into my pleasuredome of Absolute Need and finish this last phase of your crazy male self. Maldoror, you have to enter me for your own good. Besides, I've got enough Acid Porn to last twenty lifetimes."

42

"Yes, Mother."

And she opens her legs wider than a suburban house whereupon Mal walks in and prepares to write the chants that will always be the end of him.

Upon entering the secret city of Dharmagone

Mal is met by three very beautiful blond women in shiny
blue lycra jumpsuits with red anarchy signs emblazoned
over their left breasts. They approach him with glassy-eyed
smiles. He immediately recalls a dream he once had in which
three blond women (the same ones?) approach him. In the
dream they were stoned-out rockers. Déjà vu?

The tall one with icy blue eyes and lips extraordinnaire
talks first.

"Welcome to Dharmagone. We are the Andrew Sisters."

All three of them laugh and the shorter one with almost
pitchblack eyes takes hold of Mal's upper arm says,
"We're just kidding Mal. Although it's true that the Power of
Sisterhood is ultra-hot around here."

The third one, whose jumpsuit is zipped down from her
neck to her navel exposing a deep cleave of wet probability,
looks at Mal with a serious stare that'd rattle anybody.

"You're one of us Mal. We know it's not easy. You'll have
a difficult time getting through these chants because remnants of your old self, your old culture, will permeate them.
But we understand your dilemma. We act like we know
everything because we *do* know everything, or everything
that needs to be known. We have the Sexual Blood. You too
will soon walk the streets of your planet with an incredible
ability to attract and *con*-tract Sexual Blood relations with a
multitude of Others. We're very excited about absorbing
whatever amount of Otherness you can bring into the
circle."

The tall one continued: "You will find tenderness, warmth
and passion here in Dharmagone. These are the things
you've been craving. We understand that things are not
quite what you'd like them to be back on Earth."

Mal tried to answer but nothing came out.

The shorter one explained to him that his voice was going through temporary changes.

"Similar to the last change it went through during puberty," she continued, "only now it's trying to adjust itself to the sound waves of our city. You see, Mal, you're not going to sound the way you usually sound to yourself. You will sound like us in just a bit. Like Woman."

Mal immediately put a smirk on his face. What a conspiracy! He was really going to sound like a Woman! His heart started beating faster than ever. He was trying to exclaim his excitement about it all but his efforts at this were futile. Nothing was coming out.

Nor could he try a sign language. As usual, his inability to describe in detail what was happening to him and/or his surroundings made each passing moment a new discovery as regards his situation. As was always the case when lost in the labyrinthine structures of his precocious dream-apparatus, things seemed abnormal but it took forever to figure out why they felt that way. For one thing, he was no longer a body in the typical sense of the term.

He was a white gyration of light the consistency of creamed jelly. He wasn't touching the ground with feet but a whipping tail hanging below him continually snapped at the purplish-pink environment that kept pulsating all around him. He felt as human as he ever felt so his mind suggested that he was the same size as he had always been in adult life. But in actuality he was one-500th of an inch long. He was a single sperm.

"What's going to happen," said the serious one, "is this: we're going to take you into our city and let you creatively release yourself. We'll set you up with a great scenario so that you can write the horrid Y chromosomes out of your body. As soon you've successfully depleted yourself of this monster sex filament we'll inseminate you with an X chromosome that'll blow your mind. You'll have all the internal characteristics of a Woman but, once back on planet Earth, your outer Male Category will camouflage itself in the patriarchal superstructure. At that point, you'll be able to start infiltrating the systemic realities that bother you so much."

"You'll need help along the way and there are a few of us already there but the more we can register to Our Cause the better. The best way to do this is to feed certain select Others the drug Acid Porn while sharing with them your Sexual Blood. You'll be the only one on the planet capable of transfusing this Nutrience vis a vis Penetration. A dream come true, hey Mal?"

"It really is," said Mal although it didn't sound like Mal. It sounded more like a <Val>.

"Short for Valerie," said the serious one whose zipper had come undone to her pubic hair. Mal or <Val> or whoever it was was eager to go down and start nibbling on her patch of perfection.

"Why are you not an egg?" he asked her, still getting used to this very sexy feminine voice that was coming out of him.

All three of them laughed just like they did when they first started teasing him.

"We *are* eggs," said the short one. "We've just taken on these casual appearances to turn you on. Who'll get off on an ovulating eggcream?"

They laughed at that too but <Val> seemed confused.

"Oh," said the tall one: "he's confused. Don't worry <Val>, you'll get rid of that sperm get-up just as soon as we can get you in the amnion. The amnion will coat and protect you. It's really just a hyped-up image-maker. You're going to be beautiful, that's easy to see."

"See that neon entryway over there," asked the serious one.

"Yes."

"That's the entrance to the Fallopian Tube although round here we call it the Fetal Memory Shaft. Everything you'll ever remember after death will happen to you while you're in there. An Amnion Station is set-up right at the entryway to encode you for Journey. It's very simplistic, I know, but that's what makes wacky science-fiction so much fun! It's the kind of stuff kids love."

"I don't want to be a kid."

"Oh don't worry <Val>, you won't ever feel that way again. Once you re-emerge on the planetary scene, you'll be back in adult human form. But in the meanwhile, the great Goddess Shakti, our highest Being, she awaits you in a Womb of Her Own and there's only one way to get there. Are you game?"

"Do I really have a choice," he asked but the question was rhetorical and he realized it as he asked it. He got this cute look on his face and the three egg-women started quietly molesting him. He felt like a kid again.

With the help of the three egg-women <Val> flagellated himself to the Amnion Station. He still found himself feeling the need to see his outer category as Male. This is how others would perceive him no matter what kind of changes he'll have gone through internally. So when the attendant at the Amnion Station asked the group who this sperm was it was <Val> who answered:

"I'm Valerie. From where I came I'm Maldoror. The difference between the two is how they *present* themselves. I have come to see the Goddess Shakti."

The attendant was kind of sardonic.

"Yeah, Pal, or <Val>, or whoever you are, we *all* want to see the Goddess Shakti. But it ain't that easy. Lemme see yer papers."

"Papers?" <Val> looked at the three blond women who had escorted him.

"He doesn't have any papers," said the serious one. "He's paperless."

"Which is why he's going to see Shakti," said the shorter one. "She'll imbibe him with mediumistic love-energy so that he'll finally unwrite himself. The Unwritten do not need any papers. They are…"

"Silence," said the attendant now acting very stern.

Everyone stiffened up and said nothing.

"Silence," the attendant said again, this time more sweet. "They are Silence. I'm just giving you a hard time <Val>. It's probably because I'm nervous for you. I've got this weird maternal thing for anyone that even *looks* like a sperm. What can I say? It's in my genes or something. And so I start getting real schizo whenever something strange like this starts to happen. Oh dearest <Val>, I'm so nervous for you. Who knows if we'll ever see you again? I'm, I'm not sure this is so good for you. But I guess it's not my place to decide. Anyway, here's the Genetic Encoder. It's made by G.E., get it? Oh god, why do I even *pretend* to have no interest in these things? It's like I can lose total control any second. Like now. But I won't. It's just not right. Wait a second: I need to gain my composure here. For godsakes, I'm a professional. Okay. I'm okay. You are too <Val>. Don't worry. Step inside the encoder and a balloon of liquid data will protect you and your partner on the Journey. You'll have to choose one of these three women as your partner. Please decide quickly since the hormonal walls of the Great Mother's Womb are just now preparing for your arrival."

<Val> felt his heart beat faster. He couldn't decide.

"Please, <Val>," said the serious one whose zipper was all the way down. The top of her cunt was hanging out the edges of her jumpsuit.

"It will be her," said <Val>.

"Good," said the attendant, "now if you both will please step inside the G.E. this will only take a few seconds to get started."

Both <Val> and his partner said goodbye to the attendant and the other two egg-women who had tears streaming down their faces.

"Emotions," said <Val>. "Emotions will conquer all."

And into the Genetic Encoder they went.

49

Inside the G.E. they felt nothing. They were systematically merging into one cell whereupon the first words <Val> said to his partner were:

"I don't even know your name."

"I'm Isadora."

"Huh, that's funny, my father's name was Isadore."

"It happens."

They were lying side by side as an envelope of tingling fluid encased them. They dug this immensely. It was the kind of feeling you wished would last forever.

"I wish this would last forever."

"It can't. Nothing lasts forever."

"Okay, you be the pragmatic one. I'll be the irrational nutcase."

"No, I wanna be the irrational nutcase."

"Do people really talk like this?"

"It depends."

"Depends on what?"

"On what you mean by people. I'm not a person."

"Then what are you?"

"I'm an amphibian. I'm an androgynous sex cell. I'm out to turn people into feelings."

"I'm feelings myself. Me myself an I. A feeling."

"Emotions rule. I can feel it in my skin."

"You don't have any skin."

"Well, actually I do. It's the skin of feeling. Wanna feel?"

"Sure."

Someone copped a feel.

"Wow."

"That's incredible, isn't it?"

"It really is. What did you say that was?"

"Sin. I mean skin. The art of feeling."

"It's not an art! C'mon…"

"No, really, it is. Feel again."

Someone feels again.

"*Nug.*"

"Huh?"

"*Nug. Nug nug nug.*"

"Those are my tubers. A whole forest of tubers awaits us, I'm sure. I've heard about it. There are stories."

"*Nuhg.*"

"*Nuhh. Nugh Nuhhh.*"

Someone tried to ask a question but felt a splitting pain divide itself right down their middle. "Are you there?" It was as if something were talking to itself. There was no answer. She had essentially become him. And him her. Before they could even begin to recuperate memory loss and/or the pangs of desire they had felt just after they went into the G.E. there started this wrenching gut-pulling sensation like they were coming apart at the seams. It was growing pains.

They were becoming a cluster bomb of meaning.

They were becoming a political subject.

The pain was too excruciating. In this instance, pre-birth was as bad as prolonged dying. Being born was learning how to deal with pain. Death: the feeling of death begins thirty minutes after you attach yourself to whatever happens to be there when your time comes. Time comes. And the world suffers because of it.

Rolling into the sleep of death at a rate faster than Night's heart wound up and ready to scream out the anger that depicts life's nuisance. Fool babykins chubby cheeks dove's-ass hair tiny feet teeny-weeny fingers big goofy eyes. Clusterbomb of meaninglessness trying to develop a political agenda before it's too late. A blastocyst of memory pus waiting for the magic shot of Nutrience.

"Nutrience kills."

Who said that?

Something sleeps. Divides clusters divides seeps. Five days and nothing but sleep. The sphere of encoded Something that globulates in a liquid dementia unable to realize its potential warring powers creates yet another split. And another. Each split furthering the agenda. Fragmentation. Choice. Impulse. Power. Sex. Money. Death.

Being born is not yet ready to happen. Never ready to happen. Would rather nestle in the thick rich sugar of Mama Womb's makeshift walls. Where the journey ideally ends. Where Mama waits. Love Goddess with a gender agenda. Shakti. Shake it baby, shake it.

"I'm coming."

"I'm coming."

"I'm coming."

The future seeps visionary lunacy. Child demon speaks:

"I'm coming."

"I'm really coming now . . ."

"ughhh"

"""""""""""

"nuhhhhhhhhhhg."

Green cat eyes awaken to the sound of purring.

Shakti is fingering herself.

"Hi, <Val>. Welcome to my home. Wanna fuck?"

"Is that you Mother?"

Her slutty cat eyes appeal.

She's the Medicine Woman all over again.

"I have a great idea, <Val>. Let's come *together*."

<Val> feels himself salivating.

"You must be tired. You have a placenta moustache under your nose."

"Who are you?"

"I'm Nowhere. Call me Shakti if you want."

"I *want* to write my tunes. And every time I even attempt to do it, you appear. Is it something else I want and just don't know it?"

"Not really. It's all one in the same. You know what you want. And you'll get it. That much is obvious."

"So what's the story?"

"What do you mean?"

"Why am I here? What's the purpose?"

"Don't look for purpose <Val>. You're stalling, that's all. Your quill is ill. But that disease is not just the player malfunctioning. It's something else. It has to do with your desire to create life viss a vis a medium appropriate to your era of cultural history. But that doesn't mean anything to those who you share this life with so you end up resorting to age-old remedies like trying to crank out the verbal filament with supplementary noise infiltration weaving its way through the composition. No matter. I'm going to give you an opportunity to take up residence here in my womb. My womb is yours too. It's of the highest rank."

"It sure *smells* rank in here."

"Now, now, <Val>, chill out. Take a chill pill. You're tired. I'd be tired too if I just spent five days absorbing an entire Other creature who then after total absorption started splitting up on me. You're my baby <Val>. I'm here to nurture you. If all you wanna do is write music and live peacefully then that's what we'll do."

"But I thought the gig was up."

"What do you mean?"

"I mean nine months and I'm outta here, right?"

"Well, I mean, I guess you could . . ."

"Oh c'mon, Shakti, play me straight. Nine months and . . ."

". . . and you decide what you want. I'll only give birth to you if you want it that way. Otherwise, we'll fake a miscarriage and you'll stay inside me forever."

"Really?"

"Really."

"But that's what I want! It really is!! I've already made up my mind!!"

"Give it some time <Val>. Fer Chrissakes, you just got in here."

"Okay. When can I start working?"

"Well, I've set you up with a digital-audio workstation over in the Creative Wing of the Womb. It's the perfect studio environment. It's just around that glitch over there. Don't worry about the static. You're equipped to pass right through it. If you need anything let me know."

For a moment it seemed as though there were enough space and leaking sugar walls to keep him going forever. But deep inside he knew it would never last. This was no picnic he was on. He had to get those Y chromosomes out of him in whatever way the process deemed necessary. It was time to write the songs.

PRACTICE

Rugged exercise, specious gymnastics.

—Lautréamont

LE CHANTS DU MALDOROR

TO BEGIN WITH

The first thing that comes to mind as I start these chants is the time I used to take my daily walk through a narrow alley in the center of my town. Each day a slender adolescent girl would follow me at a respectful distance along that alley, watching me with sympathetic and curious eyes. She was very tall for her age and had long black hair parted in the middle. Her yellow tiger eyes pierced me from behind as if they had attached themselves on my shoulder and would not shake off lest I gave her my attention at which point she'd take them back and share her entire figure with me.

Her body was like that of a woman twice her age and she could not escape the fact that her own motordesire was revving itself up for me each and every day I passed her. Her mother, an ugly old woman with pins and curlers always in her hair, would grab at the child and drag her back into the garden-level flat in which they lived. I'd hear the mother whip the poor thing yelling at her for her indolence. I felt sorry for the girl and didn't know what to do.

Once this girl walked ahead of me on the street and everytime I tried to pass her she jutted in front of me and slowed down so that I had no choice but to check her out. She was amply proportioned from the rear view and finally, as I was about to fall over myself with possible lustful recrimination, she turned around abruptly and asked me my name.

"I have no name," I told her.

This piqued her curiosity even more. She said that everybody had a name and if I didn't have one then I was weird.

"Yes," I said, "I am weird. I am stranger than the cosmos that produces me. And yet," I looked at her with all the guilt of a criminal who knows he's about to encroach the illegal boundary once again, "you're even weirder. You're insane."

She rolled her eyes up toward the heavens and her tongue lolled about the edges of her thick pouty lips.

"Look at you," I continued, "you're not even human. You have lost all sense of yourself as a human figure. You distort your face for me as if I were a painter ready to dissect the shapelessness of your being."

She looked me up and down unsure as to who I was. My lost identity fed her appetite even more than she originally thought it would. She bit her bottom lip and her eyes sunk low and placed themselves on my crotch.

"What are you looking at?"

"I'm thinking what it would be like."

"You shouldn't be thinking those things. You're a child."

"Yes, I know. But my mind won't let me think otherwise. I have seen pictures on TV in magazines. I know what's there and yet I have not had the opportunity to really make it happen for me. In my mind I have often wondered what it would be like. And with you, a total stranger, I think it could happen. It's happened before."

"How could it have happened before? You just said . . ."

"I lied. I always lie. I'm a liar. I would lie to *you* if you'd let me be the one who made it happen."

60

I told her it was impossible. Blood and hate filled my brain. I was incapable of love but knew she'd be after me nonetheless. This was what made it so difficult.

"I will not tell a soul. Nobody knows this but you and me. I don't even care about it, really, but I *have* to find out for myself what *making it happen* is all about. There will come a time when it means something to me and then I'll start thinking things through. But now this is who I am and you're Nobody. I'll pretend you don't even exist."

This last seemed very sincere and was the only way I could even begin thinking about her. She had somehow known that by acting as if I didn't exist, she could ignite whatever possible interest I might have had in her. I told her I was incapable of love.

"Love isn't real," she said. "*This* is real," and she cupped my crotch with her sweaty palm.

Who knows what she possibly could have been thinking? There was always the chance that she was older than she at first seemed. Perhaps she was the older sister of the one I saw following me with her eyes those other days. But this is ridiculous. Speculation tends to obscure the view. She was trying to unzip my fly.

"No," I said. "Not here. Not this alleyway. Someone will see us."

She took me inside the monkeyhouse at the playground as if she knew no one would be there.

"No one's ever here," she said. "The few kids who live in this neighborhood are tired of being monkeys. They've decided it's better to stay home and watch TV."

Taking her head between my hands, gently and caressingly, I watched her easily absorb my genitals. She was like a little lost animal who had finally found a home...

STONED BLACKBIRD

Alone on a hiking trail depositing fragmentary remembrance of things past, the hot connection makes itself known to me. Drowning in the intense heat of this rapid sexual flush, I sense an imaginative impulse growing deep inside my being. This impulse is to dream up a new rendition of my battered psyche-self always getting lost on its way toward slippery language experience. Without thinking things through, I find myself consciously redirecting this impulse to an unknown void whose source is now *becoming* me.

This void will be the only residence I feel at home in, it will be Her residence, although I'll always be unsure of who she is, of Her exact nature.

Countless names will imbibe her. An arbitrary listing of possibilities makes itself known to me as I go through an amalgamation of previous sexual experiences that highlight an array of fornicating personalities who are identified as Virginia, Gertrude, Djuna, Moondata, Karen, Susan, Suzanne, Bett, Fanny, Ramona, Yolanda, Fox, Mezz, Zulu, J, Nathalie, Angela, Distension, Morbidity, Moire, Semblance, Treblinka, Tribeca, Horniness, Voluptuous Val, Malformation, Heavy Sensation and Motor Cups.

Yet here on the trail, lost in the wilderness of potential bliss, Fern Canyon (another deep gorge of streaming possibility high on grass wet as history), solemn escapade, futile attempt at setting up a hypothesis as to why I exist, an anomaly who encultures the promiscuous oil of redundancy, slick ligatures of lubrication searching the availability of some circumference of pleasure dead set on ending primary source functions.

An aberration, or, rather, an apparition, the madwoman comes sailing past me in a dance of dry death yet her native fecundity at breast and spinning rear axle make the chokecherry bushes drip their dewy residue of mistified knowledge. Seeping out an aura from all known portholes of chemical dispersement, she readily acknowledges my meager presence by encircling me inside her whirlwind of lunar energy and experience as it showcases a newfound brilliance my mindset must immediately focus on.

Her gown, torn in several places, flutters about her bony and filthy legs. Her face resembles no human countenance. There's absolutely nothing human about her except her hair which is a bundle of black sea vegetables swept back by the insufferable wind. Her breath reeks of cognac and she wastes no time in letting drop her dirty rags of phrases whose intention, I'm sure, is to disrupt the flow of my walk and set me on an errant agenda.

"I saw, with wonder and surprise, this darling little maypole of a boy, actually, he wasn't little and he wasn't a boy, he was…well, he was something outside of himself, it was as if he were no longer the person his body made him out to be and, oddly enough, that turned *him* on. You understand? He was turned on to *himself*, but obviously not *as* himself, it was as though he were of a different set of circumstances, an alternative series of experiences, perhaps internal, who can say for sure, and these experiences *must* have created an opening somewhere on the inside of his soul because as I say he was very much the normal young giant one finds all over these forests."

I tried to get a word in edgewise but this madwoman would not let go.

"The first thing I did for him was kneel. I leaned against my knees slowly digging into the dead leaves and dirt of the path we found each other on. Slowly I rocked forward on this patch of everlasting earth, each rock forward accompanied by a swift dart of my liquor-saturated tongue begging him to put the prodigious stiffness of his rockhard being into my craving-for-it slut-breath mouth. My throat was on fire with whiskey and the cognac and the deeply inhaled joints of metapleasure rolled by God Himself. I begged him to put the motherfucker clear to the back of my esophagus so that I could completely shut myself up to the point of never breathing again. I wanted my whole world to end and by cramming that polished velveteen ivory tower of swollen intensity right into what was succinctly my mortal mouth, I would possibly die with his megalomaniacal prominence stabbing my hidden depths: using his vastly overproduced bulge of macro-heaven loaded with unending amounts of bull sperm, he would stab and puncture, stab and puncture, stab and puncture, continuously, until there'd be no doubt about his Manhood, he would have eventually lacerated my cancer-ridden lungs. I wanted him to make me bleed inside. Inside where the death of identity had finally made itself a home in my heart. The beating begging heart of my directives, sir…"

(She was on her knees. Rocking back and forth with a fiery tongue dangling for meat. The pure materiality of my mongrel meat. I could not imagine a way out of this. There was no way to get around it. This was one of the unwritten requirements. The writing out of myself in stark nakedness: being born: flesh alive with searing consciousness erecting the Sexual Blood now in formation...)

The madwoman continued: "I never thought myself to be in anyway a slut or a bored housewife, I'm not an egocentric workaholic career track robot trying to run away from the demands of my feminine essence, you'll never find me hanging out in sleazy bars looking for someone who'll take me with a buzz on, never. And yet, kneeling before this incredible hulk of well-maintenanced manhood had me reeling. His length and breadth, now proud and salient like a natural curiosity done up in purple and blue flagrancy, made me deign him the new Earth God. I have never wanted anything so bad in my life. I had had it all. Everything: family, home, car, country house, good looks, partiality, everything. But one thing I had not ever had nor knew I had access to had only I ventured into the deep woods to find, was he, the well-stocked stud of all my hedonistic hallucinations. I wanted to *become* him by taking his abnormally huge and thick cock in my mouth, harness him there in the back of my throat where his scalding horse sperm would come pouring into my throat filling me with millions of potential ponies galloping throughout my bloodstream. I was bleeding the soft mane of desire. He *had* to come over to me..."

My zipper was undone and my enormous cock was bobbing wildly, as if it were trying to find what direction my soul were heading in. Since it never stopped bobbing I never got a good take on where exactly it was going. Directionless, perhaps, but a nomadology of absolute presence forever-in-transition emanated from my skin. I was HERE. HERE was where I had come. HERE was what brought me to HER. Together, HER, HERE, right now, my dick bobbing directionless in search of a soul. She was a soul.

I was too high mettled to not begin saturating her with my heat. This melding of energies in a soldered conjunction of madness and pleasure was the one thing I felt most akin to. Was it necessary? What was the feeling inside my gut that made me perform opportunistic juts of my skeletal frame in such a way as to fill her mouth with the materiality of my machine? My meat was now a machine whose heat transgressed all foregone conclusions. Which is why, I temporarily justified, I continued to shake myself in an uncontrollable manner. I was nothing but the preponderance of meat…

DESIRE GNAWING AT
CONSCIOUSNESS NEEDING

I formulated my next discursive passage. I was sincerely starting to lose myself in a white hot flash of chemical decomposition which was my soul burning with The Need. The Absolute Need. Moral or Immoral, Mortal or Immortal, the more I thought about it the more mordacious I became. I was writing myself out of my old element in hopes of attaining that precious state of Womanhood I desperately desired. The surrounding sugar walls of the womb I inhabited were leaking onto me and I was absorbing the transformative superfluids in hopes of flushing the Male Category out of my biological system.

For practice, I became a woman. It was the last girl I fucked. Her horny desperate spirit is the fuel that drives this motorized song.

"120 MINUTES"

[The MTV special alternative rock program was on full blast: "Sex sells sex (yeah)/ You sold me too."]

J was a virgin but not for very long. She was sick and tired of watching MTV play with her amorous psyche. The tight jeans commercial with the perfectly-cut fashion model baring his naked torso wasn't a turn-on so much as it was an invitation to participate in a society-wide sexual revolution that just didn't exist. Something like a sexually suggestive feeling was transpiring inside her desiring body.

Her desiring body was an *activity* looking for a way out. The only way out was through her orifices. She was sick and tired of being the latest fashion. She wanted to be an active cunthole. She wanted to be perceived as an open mouth. Her secretive side wanted nothing more than an experienced older man cleaning out her asshole with his hard old man dick. She was too clogged up. She needed a flaming hot male debunking agent. She became obsessed with her imagination and the things it would fantasize.

*

J's conviction was to get experienced. She visited her mother's friend Angela.

Angela was delighted to help J. As soon as J had come to her house to visit, Angela insisted that J stay for the afternoon, for there were some friends of hers expected to drop by and the sexual theatrics would begin. Not only would J learn the secrets of sexually-fulfilling *activity*, she would expose herself to the supplementary philosophical speculation that attached itself to such *activity*.

Angela: "You must feel good about your*self*, dear J, or else the aura you emit will have an adverse effect on the sexual partners you interact with. The best way to do that is to strip yourself to skin and bones, then, when you've adjusted to room temperature, start feeling yourself up and down your body. *Your body is your self.* The two are *only* reconcilable. When a fissure develops between the two as if abstinence or celibacy were taking totalitarian control over your desire to reach out and grab hold of the thing that needs to penetrate you, then you've become drugged by an evil doctrine of energy that suppresses the human impulse toward passion. Although you need not think about it. Just start jerking yourself off. Go on...."

J stood before Angela as if she needed some help taking off her clothes but Angela didn't move to help her because that would ruin the whole lesson. J, who had only felt herself in the privacy of her little girl's pink bedroom, was now in the master bedroom. She was in the master bedroom with a burning urge to fuck anything that walked but she was also innocent and inexperienced and wasn't sure if jerking off in front of her mother's friend was the appropriate thing to do. The strange discipline of corporate-inspired appropriation had effected her entire life. Desire was a sales-tactic invented by marketing wizards who knew her and girls like her to be easily influenced slaves of popular media. She felt lucky to be with (know) Angela and really wanted to take advantage of Angela's openness. Yet, she still had trouble undressing.

*

J had a question:

"I thought *men* had appendages to jerk. Women, though, we have things to flick or rub or pinch or softly twist. How do we jerk?"

Angela was proud of her star pupil. She'd get very far very fast. The idea was to look vulnerable. Angela didn't say anything. She just looked like she had fallen in love with J's tantra potential. She wanted to plant her head in between J's legs and suck out all the little girl juices that wanted desperately to release themselves. But she just looked at J and

69

remained silent. She was staring at J's still-covered cunt.

J finally got the message and slowly took off her tight jeans. She was hesitant but had a sexy almost slutty smile on her face as if this scene had been rehearsed many times before. Perhaps it had. J's dreams were full of such scenes.

(J once dreamed her younger sister, Nathalie, was home from school sick and J decided to play hookey so that her mother wouldn't feel like she had to stay home from work. Mother told J to take care of both her sister and herself and she'd try to get off work early in the afternoon. That morning, J, taking advantage, told Nathalie that she had to take her temperature and Nathalie said okay but could she put it in her butt instead of under her armpit. J got that same sexy somewhat slutty smile on her face and said Sure. Nathalie's butt was a small firm globe of endless need that J starting jerking off. She took the thin thermometer and coated it with Vaseline. Then she started moving it in and out of Nathalie's asshole, in and out, in and out, in and out, first very fast so that it tickled, then, without pause, very slowly, a very slow, deliberate, slightly obscene m:o:v:e:m:e:n:t...Nathalie had a glazed look in her eyes and her mouth hung open with spit drooling out of it. If the scene had been in a painting, the oil would've been smeared so that the children looked like half-dead monsters on the verge of screaming orgasm.

After J had slowly fucked her sister with the thermometer for more than thirty minutes, Nathalie fell asleep for almost three hours. When Nathalie woke up their mother had just arrived home from work (early, like she said she would). Mother asked Nathalie how she felt and Nathalie said she felt much better and would like to go out and play. J was in the living room watching MTV. In her memory of the dream, J remembers her floating camera eye moving all throughout the house as if she were a hovering god of intention whose origin was still unknown. Her aerial view of the little girl watching TV frightened her. That lonely inexperienced emotionally undeveloped mass of goose flesh was herself, nobody.)

J wasn't lost in revery. She couldn't afford to be. Reconstructing and patching up her dreams with the haze of phantom scenes she forever passed through was a way of engineering herself through her normal day-to-day combat with the adolescent war zombies she called her friends. Today, though, was the most important day of her life. She was totally naked now and was feeling up her breasts. Her body was rippling with sensation. She wanted to take the blood of dreams and spread it over her desiring body. She was nothing but *activity*, a happening slice of forbidden fruit glistening with its own juices.

*

The drug dealer in town (known by all as The Horseman), was the first guest to arrive at Angela's house. J was stretched out on Angela's kingsize bed playing with herself.

Horseman: "What have we got here? Why, it's young J, the hottest high-school chick in all of town. The beauty of it all !!"

Angela felt shunned.

"Horseman," she said, "perhaps I can distract you for a moment. Remember *me*, Angela, the woman you might've come to see?"

Horseman: "Oh dear love, how horrid of me. I worship the carpet you spill your wine on…I am the moral equivalent of the ashtray you smolder your dope in…I humbly beg your

71

forgiveness…(and he came over to her burying his head in between her open legs sucking on the bloody meat that lay there like an all-you-can-eat buffet at Furr's Cafeteria)

"Watch me J," Angela instructed, "watch me respond to the Horseman as he eats the bloody nature that nurtures him."

J, who was still jerking herself off, saw the Horseman (who all the girls in school knew as a sexual deviant who could get just about anything he wanted because of his killer headstash) sink himself into Angela's menstruating pussy.

"The blood of a poet," said the Horseman as he came up for air, stringy blood hanging from his chin, then, "the blood of a *poetess* discharging itself into the abyss of uncertain knowledge, that's me J, I'm the unknown, I'm the brief moment of intoxication that spurs on the blurry night of ideal narcosis, you too dear J will lose yourself in the act of finding *me*, the holy Horseman streaking through your veins of irreconcilable need…"

The Horseman reached into his shirt pocket and pulled out a piece of brown Pak. He lightly tossed it toward J who caught it right in her mouth and swallowed. It was terrible bitter. She said something like "yuk, yuuuuk." But in moments she was flashing.

*

Angela begged the Horseman to pummel.

The Horseman obliged his mistress by ramming deep and hard. His eyes lit with infinitesimal streaking. He was lost in the pleasure of finding himself between her womanly thighs. J was wasting away on the heavy Pak shit.

Now J was slurring. She said: "…shit, Horsey, ride *me*, *my* cunt needs a fix, you can ride *me* Horsey, you can *right* me…"

Horseman rearranged (with Angela) the positioning of all involved by helping the blown-away J to her knees and putting her in the doggy-style position. While he got at her from behind and broke open the walls of cherryhood that had pitted her against all future experience of pain and despair, Angela snuck up behind him and was fingering/licking his asshole. Horseman, a big prick preceding him, pummeled and ruled over the half-dead J. When he needed to come, he yelled "I've got to shoot it in her" and Angela yelled at him to pull it out and put it in J's mouth so that she could taste the sweet love the Horseman was capable of producing. He did so and J's tongue slurped up the globs of goo he uncontrollably shot into her precious mouth. Angela, desiring J's pussy, went in between the young girl's legs to finish the cum-job Horseman had started. She licked and nibbled and sucked at J's cunt for a good long while until J completely lost track of herself in the midst of all this (coming) (sensation streaming through her veins) (the drug intensifying the pleasure). The Horseman was licking Angela's asshole.

*

J had to go home for dinner. The Horseman had already departed.

Angela: "I hope you got a lot out of today's session."

J: "I'm cool baby, real cool. I dig that shit totally. It fucked me up good. You think Horseman got any more shit I can buy from him? It did me *right.*"

Angela: "What about the sex? You just got your cherry popped...."

J: "Shit was okay, I mean I dug the Horseman coming in

73

my mouth but that bloody pussy shit's for the birds. You can keep your bloody pussy. I think I need Horseman. Horseman's got a hold on me."

*

Mother wanted to know why J looked so haggard.

"Shit, Mom, I just fucked and sucked the Horseman. I'm *cooked*."

Mother, not wanting to hear anything, said she didn't understand.

"Shit, Mom, you frigid bitch. Go out and get laid. You work too much. *Now* you understand?"

Mother wasn't listening and so therefore said she still didn't understand but Nathalie who had been silent and who felt jealous of both her mother and her sister said she went swimming today.

J: "Shit, Nathalie, you wanna swim? Go fuck the Horseman. He'll swim right up into your soul and back. Let's go find him." And she got up and left the house.

Mother finished her microwaved dinner.

Nathalie went to the TV to see what was on. It was still MTV.

*

J was thinking *horsey*.

"I'm finally what I always wanted to be: penetrable. Anything big and strong can permeate my being. The power shift isn't a demographic happening. It's a narcotic that streaks through my psychopharmakinetic bloodline. I'm a slut who's *hooked* on the outlaw of my dreams, the Horseman."

By going through slight withdrawals (and slipping into gradual depression that she had no idea was slowly taking over her brand-name consciousness), J was becoming something she had unsuspectingly potentialized by being born into this crazy mixed-up world of bare bones love and corruption. She was becoming a whore.

"I'm a cheap slut who has given up MTV in favor of endless drugs and fucking. I need Horseman's dick because he's got the brown Pak that racks my brain. My head hurts unless I'm totally cool on the Pak shit with sweaty Horseman railing me hard from behind. All the textbook dress-rehearsals they throw at me in school are useless unless I experiment with my soul. I must find Horseman. His ability to radicalize discourse is what I've always wanted in a man. A man I never thought could exist."

J walked back to Angela's accessible crash-pad. She didn't even bother knocking on the door. She went straight to the master bedroom, the place where this philosophical wandering had reached critical mass.

*

The door to Angela's master bedroom was open. The sounds coming out of it were the normal oohs and ahhs fuck me hard in the cunt sounds one is used to hearing in such active parts of the household. J stood at the threshold watching some strange man cram his meteor inside Angela's spacious galaxy.

Angela: "Oh fuck! Fuck me August! Fuck my brains out!!"

August: "I'm fucking you!! Cheap slut!! Dirtiest cunt in the solar system!! Pussy degenerate!! Cosmic Cunt-bitch!!"

75

This sort of thing went on for ten or twelve minutes until the two entanglements simultaneously exploded love-cum-sighs of relief.

Together: "Aiyyyyyeeeeeuuuugggghhhhhhhhhh!!!!!!"

August collapsed on top of Angela and they both breathed very heavily for a few minutes. Angela ran her fingers through August's thick curly hair. She called him Love.

J cleared her throat loud enough for the two fuckmates to hear her. Her presence was unquestionably accepted. Angela got a shit-eating grin on her face and motioned to J to come to the bed.

Angela: "Dear J, you've returned. Brave woman. Happy (w)hole who needs another fix. Grand August has arrived for supper. Why not feed him your recently excavated twat?"

J looked at August who also had the shit-eating grin on his face too. She rubbed her stomach and sang "yummy yummy yummy I got love in my tummy...and I think I'm gonna...puke..."

And she ran to the john and heaved up a mess of green insides.

She washed her mouth out and brushed her teeth with one of the toothbrushes she found. Then she came back out and hopped into bed. August and Angela were lying next to each other reading books (just like J remembered her parents doing together before they got divorced and her father left never to come back again).

J: "Excuse me folks, but I thought we were going to feed August his dinner. Has the plan changed?"

The adults, acting like parents, weren't paying any attention whatsoever to her inquiring mind. They just read their books. Occasionally one of them would speak to the dead air saying something like "yes, darling, and have a good day in school tomorrow."

J grew furious: "I'm not going to school. I'm going to fuck. I'm going to eat good drugs and get my pussy satiated. My burning walls of confusion need to melt down. I need to break on through to the other side. Poetry won't do it. MTV won't do it. New clothes won't do it. Nothing does it except stoned sex. That's what I live for."

The parents paid her no mind. August fell asleep with the book in his lap.

J demanded Angela's attention. She wanted to know who the crude brute in bed with her was.

Angela: "It's only August. He's the lawn-mower boy. He looks older because he's been traveling and traveling ages you. Especially when you go on and on for what seems like eternity. Especially when you're a sexual genius with a fourteen-inch cock in your favor. Do you understand?"

J: "If he's the lawn-mower boy then how come I've never seen him? I thought Davey Nelson was the lawn-mower boy for our neighborhood."

Angela: "So he is. But August is a different kind of lawn-mower boy. He specializes in hedging and edging the patch of weed that grows around your pussy. Let me see your pussy."

J knew that Angela was lying to her and that as a lying cunt with no scruples to speak of she probably had a lot of money that J could steal. J figured she now needed money to support her new habit which was either The Horseman, his drug, or some combination thereof. So she did what Angela said. She took off her dress and before Angela could say anything else was straddling the older woman's face. Angela's tongue responded favorably.

After Angela made J come (her first cunnilingus come), she turned half of her face onto her pillow, closed her eyes and fell asleep. That's when August stretched awake. The first thing his eyes saw was J who was still dripping come on Angela's half-exposed face.

August: "You look wet. Cheap slut? Degenerate pussy? Cosmic ca-ca-ca-caphony of candied cunt? For me?"

Before he could fully spread his shit-eating grin J straddled him too and said "Eat me lawn-mower boy before I blow your brains out."

August ate the succulent J. She came. And she came again. Then she blew his brains out.

J wandered the streets dreaming a new philosophy that would re-energize the spiritual bankruptcy of her disintegrated culture. She thought of home, MTV, dinner, the brown Pak shit, Horseman, running away to Amerika. She was *in* Amerika.

*

J wandered aimlessly. *That* was crux of her new philosophy. To occasionally fragment the unintentional movement of thought in an improvised setting of language and experience that *might* develop a pattern (of seeing) thus enabling the possibility of enjoying a new unforeseen version of herself, the wanderer who debilitates the stagnant parent culture.

She was no authority on the subject but she was uncertain of everything and that meant she was pure. The membrane of existence tore at her cunt's edge. That's where she would lose herself, forever.

Walking was wondering and feeling alone was sexually coming into being. She jerked off behind a building. She rolled down a hill. The moon was an obsolete symbol that seemed to appear in her field of vision just to bug her. She needed *horsey*.

*

J thought: "The real politik is staying alive in a world's sense embargo." She now realized that the cargo she carried with her everywhere she went was the most illegal contraband unprotected by the law. It was her *self*, the woman in waiting. Waiting for the child within that would wed her to death.

Horseman's junky child of emblematic death-desiring was beginning to approximate a sense of style and/or being within her carnal circulation. Only when it came out (*if* it came out) would it really be a living thing although the right-to-lifers would say that just by *thinking* such thoughts one was liable to be shot for treason. The reason being Reason Itself. Reason Itself was a religious bone coated in unctuous love fluid that J wanted to gyrate on. Religion made her lubricate. Lubrication was her religion. She would wet her pants just thinking about hard cocks filling young cunts with experiential wonder.

Her aborted poetic self (the one she lost in front of the TV microwave gas pumps McDonalds lunch counter at school) was coming back in the form of a ghost. The devastatingly intense ghostwriting that permeated her imagination was an ethereal hieroglyphics that masked itself in the code of a dissoluting day desperately seeking a compassionate night. J started murmuring to herself

can't see (my eyes hurt)
can't hear (the noise outside rapes me of serene love energy)
can't taste (contaminant debris strays toward my tongue darting)

79

can't feel (too much money monkeying on my back)
can't smell anything but the pollution drowning my sea breeze

*

J sees her skin change colors and knows the sun is dressing her in its brand-name light. Although she hasn't slept well and feels fatigued beyond dreaming, she feels ready to do something charged and energetic. She puts her clothes back on and starts walking through the field she spent the night in.

The morning freshness smells damp. Her cunt stinks. The sounds of early commuters cranking cars triggers her mind toward more motor-desiring. The concept "motor-desiring" enters her head but she doesn't know from where. It's the first she's ever heard of it.

The feel of a cup of hot coffee in her hand twists her mind toward something close to clarity. She thinks about stealing some old lady's purse so she can pocket some cash and take the next bus out of town.

The taste of yesterday is still on her tongue and she wonders if she should say goodbye to The Horseman before she splits. He might want to go with her. He might want to change his life with her.

*

J couldn't find The Horseman's number. She was looking under H. Then she remembered that Horseman was his pseudonym and that his real name was Don One. So she looked under One and found his number.

The phone rang over twenty times before he picked it up.

"Hello?"

"Hey."

"Hey is for horses."

"And Horsemen. Why not admit it?"

"Who is this?"

"*Admit it.*"

"Admit what? Who is this?"

"Admit that you love me and want to run away with me?"

"Are you out of your...who *is* this? Marcia? Is that you?"

J was stunned. Who was Marcia? Not Marcia Brady. Not her worst enemy. Not that rich cunt who had everything. Not Horseman too.

Silence on both ends of the receiver. J, envious bitch that she was, was ready to cry. (She was every girl in high-school personified in a letter, J, for jealousy jackrabbitt jaculate jaded jailbait jism-jointed juvenescent.) She couldn't resist (stop herself) from asking Horseman the question etched on her one-track mind.

"You mean Marcia Brady?"

"Yes I mean Marcia Brady...uh...who is this?"

He sounded more resolute. He was connecting.

"Now do you remember?"

"J, baby, it's you. How's your head?"

"My head's fine. It's my cunt that's all messed up. It reeks mostly of you, egghead. Why not come and get me?"

"Where are you?"

"At Kroger's."

"Wait there. I'll be right there."

*

Horseman came over to her on a souped-up Yamaha.

"Open your mouth," he said and she obeyed.

He threw in a piece of Pak.

By the time they were back at his dirty stinkhole of a pad, she was buzzing.

Horseman took off his pants. Pulled out his mangy whanger and had J kneel before it. As she was about to approach it for immediate sucking, he stopped her and pulled out a pamphlet from his leather jacket's inside pocket. With much (imaginary) fanfare he began to read from the pamphlet:

"ONE MORE TIME AMERIKA, BEFORE YOU TOTALIZE YOURSELF INTO A SINGLE HORRIFIC CONGLO-MERATION...my countrymen, my little cuntlings, all juvenile delinquents who feel the need to turn the telecom-munications revolution into an endless love free-for-all, we have seen our leaders continuously disregard the rising apathy at the ballot-box. They think they know what is best for us. They refuse to concede. Power has immobilized them. Money has hardened them. They are the caulk that keeps our shitters together. I say *shit on them!* We can do better than this! We are free and accomplished souls who regard our bodies with the highest sexual regard!! The spirit of our dematerialization into nothing but burning desire-energy is the code we shall crumble them with!!!

"We have not done our duty countrymen and darling cuntlings! We have allowed them to crawl from the wreck-age and find their fragmented columns of disgust!! The foundations they built an empire of corruption and greed on are within their cumulative grasp!! We must cut off their hands and make sure they never feel the power to grow into obnoxious monsters again!! We must guillotine their heads so that thoughts of ruling our bodies and texts of experiential knowledge never have say over our lives again!! THIS IS THE

MOST CRUCIAL TIME IN OUR SHORT HISTORY AS A NATION OF BEAUTIFUL CUNTS AND STONED-OUT CUNT-EATERS!!!

"My friends, the time has come to realize that morals should be the basis of religion and not religion the basis of morals. Our religion, forever in-the-making, must find its destination in the fictionality of our sexual selves, the beings we desperately dream of promulgating for as long as our mortality lets us!! We must be flagrant!! We must whip some sense into the passive minds of our brainwashed brethren!! WE MUST DO THIS NOW!! NO TIME TO SPARE!! TIME IS NOT ON OUR SIDE!!

"I repeat, dearest cunts and countryeaters, to be free, we must be delivered not only from the inertia that strangles our pussy government but also from the conservative nature of our faceless censors!! Reason Itself is telling you what to do with your itinerant madness!! These strange spiritual cravings that slowly creep inside your gut and force you to deal straight on with your fate are only interested in *your* getting the most intense sexual gratification you can imagine!! You must start paying attention to these hungry passions!! The answer to your prayers is not just money!! Money is available to all whores who know how to get it!! Big fucking deal!! What we need is an extra-sensorial implosion of raw gut feeling!! What we need is an endless orgasm ripping through our ultra-sensitive bodies!! The deprived soul is a disaster waiting to happen!! Don't get fooled again!! Be a true believer!! Fuck the nearest God or Goddess at hand!!

"You who have your revolutionary axes in your hand must deal the final blow to the tree of tyranny; it is not enough to nip off a few of its branches; you must pull it out by the roots! It is our duty as pornosophic love-mechanics to hasten the education of our youth! Educate them not in textbook dogma that will convert them to the cause of gross national product!! That is for slaves and stressed-out baboons who don't know what it's like to live without the next homeboy's policy fix!! Instead, teach them to unite against such silly stupidities, to forge ahead a new identity lost in the flux of mutually adhered-to love sensations!! These remarkable outcasts will awaken an entire new age of pleasure beyond joy!!

"Come my little cuntling! Dearest J! Let's eat this smelly luscious world of innate corruption!! Let's eat it, digest it, and then *excrete* it on the faces of our enemies who wish we were dead enough for them to masturbate their private hells all over our innocent faces!! Long live our starry alliance!! Long live FREEDOM!!"

*

J patiently listened to Horseman deliver his speech. She had her opinions on it but refused to say what they were. She had other things on her mind.

"Horseman, what would you say if I told you I wanted to have your baby? That I wanted us to try and make a baby thing happen in our desolate life? Would you desert me?"

Horseman started fondling himself. J was still kneeling before him.

"Horseman, what would you say if I told you that I wanted us to get married and quit drugs and have sex to make babies? Would that turn you on?"

Horseman was hard now. He was rapidly jerking his cock in the face of the young starveling.

"Horseman, what would you do if I told you I wanted to go

back to school to study more textbooks so that I could then learn what society is all about and how to make my fair share of money for the express purpose of having children so that they too could go to good schools and read textbooks that will foster *their* growth for them? Would that make you want me more than you ever wanted another human being, even Marcia Brady?"

Horseman was turning blue. His cock was harder than a cro-moly bike frame.

"Horseman, I'm about to make a very big decision that will effect our lives from here on in. This decision will eventuate the love I know we have for each other. It will be the direct result of my not being able to do what I really want to do with my life and I'll regret my life for as long as I live. I will be an Amerikan, Horseman, I will obey the gods of money-junk."

Horseman started to come all over her face. He yelled a moan so loud it woke his nearby neighbors. He was so throttled by the ejaculation that he couldn't stand up and had to fall to his knees where he stared the cum-faced J in the eyes.

"I'm not going to kill you," he said to her, softly touching her face.

"I'm not going to…" he dabbed his index finger in a spot of glistening cum and tasted it. It tasted *alive*…

THE HIDDEN AGENDA OF THE

FUCKING RICH

Nibbling on pastures of cunt with mostly tongue though some fingers and teeth. To apply the pleasure pressure. The pleasure pressure softly touching the swollen pearl drop. Making the menses come. Come into being. Rich Jewish cunt-being. Susan Shapiro's mother-of-pearl ointment swathing my sore mouth with excess love moaning in the background.

But the love isn't always there and now that she's come in my mouth Susan wants to know about my intentions. She's young. She's past adolescence so she's not so interested in experimenting with me anymore. She's not quite in her sexual prime (or what my old girlfriend Mioux-Mioux calls "sexual prime-time"). Every Monday through Friday from eight in the evening till the time her alarm clock wakes her up the next morning, her time is taken up with mostly two things: (1) sleeping off the stress easily associated with being a workaholic humanoid and having or not having money to blow on easily attainable consumer items or (2) making life miserable for herself and anybody else who happens to be schmoozing inside her tainted concave of resentment.

Shapiro flexes her muscles everytime she tries to intimidate you. She's been working out at the gym and she's damn proud of her rockhard power machine: her body cradling the child within: the baby she used to be (is this what's become of the Feminine Mystique?). She shows me the poem she just wrote right after I assisted her in orgasm. It reads

Rugged exercise, specious gymnastics
enables me to come harder than even
Nancy Reagan who's never read a book.
I may hate Men but you can't call me
a misogynist.

Sow pussy. Clit a burning cyclamen.
Orgasms that smell like tooth decay
being drilled. Susan Shapiro.

The next day she went to see my dentist. He got in her mouth and wouldn't let loose till she promised she'd go out with him. She has that effect on people. It's not so much her personality as it is the challenge her domineering presence invites. It's her tight jeans and her long red fingernails. Her dark brown eyes and penciled-in eyebrows. Beautiful smooth hands that take warm hard cocks in the grooves of her moist palms and softly jerk them off until bursting blue balls can no longer take it. Creamy cum mouthwash. She gargles. Leans her head back and gurgles again. Swallows with an ultrapersonified GULP.

She starts hanging out with my dentist because she thinks he'll make a good father and good fathers are hard to come by. Especially in *her* class. Or what she thinks is her class. It has something to do with having lots of money but still needing to accumulate debt to cook the balance sheet despite the fact that unless something completely out of her control happens instantaneously without her having a say in it, she'll always have money. Something about need, insatiability, greed, hate and death-desiring.

"But I didn't even know children were in your future."

"Look," she tells me, "we, that is to say thirtysomething

or anothers, we have to have it all. Children are part of the Big Picture. They are the crying manipulative expensive extensions of our conservative selves. I want something I can call mine. I can't call the company I work for mine. I can't call the trails I walk on mine. I can't even call the goody two-shoes environmentalism I go out of my way to support mine. Nothing is mine. Except this easily attainable stress. And without stress there's no need for sex. And sex produces children which produce more stress. Therefore I am. Get it? And by the way, why do you keep pressuring me?"

"I'm not pressuring you. I'm *pleasuring* you. There's a difference. Pleasure revolves around the individual's idiosyncratic need for a specific kind of *physicality*. You prefer to dream of some acquiescing power-trip. That's *materiality*. And that's the difference between you and me. It's so easy to see it too. Conventional reality is what you want to show to your parents. They'll approve. See? (you'll say to them), just like *you*. You're the happy extension of your family. Or maybe it's unhappy extension. Whatever. Families mitigate. They make you in their own image (and don't disregard the Godliness of that statement). Dead identity Susan. Dead, just like your father's name which I use in vain, Shapiro."

"You just say that," she was driveling. "You're not even capable of fucking me. You try to stick it in and swish it around but all you end up doing is coming. Coming isn't fucking. Fucking is something else. It's beyond fucking."

*

I realize that Susan Shapiro was not only trying to be my mother but in all probability had a direct line to the woman who actually gave birth to me. Although I had changed my

88

name sixteen times and had not spoken to my mother for over twelve years it seemed all too obvious that this was who Shapiro was. She was just a younger version.

If I continued to feel guilty about being the person I was then I'd have to remain that person. Guilt grows on you, like a cancer whose goal is to *become* you, to catastrophically suffocate you in an authorial signature. But guilt eluded me and I could be somebody else tomorrow. Actually it could happen today, right now, I could easily be Maldoror. I *am* Maldoror. An element of his spirit has fallen into me and for some reason, or in total defiance of anything remotely resembling Reason, without even trying, I won't let it out. Just taking on the name and absorbing parts of the sentiment while inmixing it with all the sediment of previous selves not to mention shorn pieces ripped from the collective-self. For each person, several *other* lives were in due process....

With self now melted into unreadable energy transgressing the nightmare of existence I had been forced to live in, there was no choice for me but to constantly remain in flux. It wasn't that I was hiding anything, some dark spot in my past. There weren't any proverbial skeletons in my closet. I was just juiced on change and if the multi-national conglomeritized network of economic fascism didn't want to change with me then that was fine too. Actually, it was desired. I desired to be different, to break away from Corpo-Slave Culture. And I was sure I could do it too.

The thing was, you see, I was sexy. So it didn't matter. Nothing mattered when you were sexy because sex sold. Sexuality sold sexuality. It was blood currency. People bought the sexuality whatever it was. If it was Don Juan TV Private Eye they'd go for that. If it was superannotated Material Girl writhing into some androgynous robot's knee while

MARK AMERIKA

moaning out her latest pop song, they'd go for that too. If you were an alien porn star whose aura emitted an unknown power-force that converted all possible negative thought into the liquid potential of positive play then that'd be cool too. Looking into my crystal-ball I saw that my own sexual future was an anonymous orgasm exploding inside a virtual sex arcade where an animated Everybody Whore was flashing drippy data right in front of my forlorn face.

Shapiro couldn't get a focus on me and not only that but I gave her the best orgasms she ever had in her life. Those two things, uncertainty of my identity and certainty of the power she felt whenever she had sex with me, drove her wild. She had a shit-conniption over our sex life and couldn't control it.

In the beginning, when she was still experimenting with the thought of just fucking me for the fun of it, she wanted to play the game as if it was nothing but too-close-to-call death ready to wipe her ass right off the face of the planet. I WAS THE DANGEROUS ELEMENT IN AN OTHERWISE COMPLACENT DO-NOTHING LIFE. I WAS THE UNKNOWN QUANTITY IN HER RISK MANAGEMENT PORTFOLIO. She was instinctively turning on the maternal organ grinder cranking out sick music for whatever amount of attention I'd give her. I was broke so all I had to give her was my attention. I'd spend hours gnawing away at her rosemary clit.

I felt the roughness of the shag carpet rubbing against my chin as I eagerly ate at her precious loins. The most perfect kosher cut I had ever tasted. As if there were grape wine oozing out of there. Upwardly mobile Mad Dog 20-20 dripping into my ready mouth. As if performing cunning lingus sessions was a new kind of Amerikan Kaddish.

I loved eating her because she really let loose that way. Her

90

whole body would do these uncontrollable shakes and contortions. Sometimes she would stiffen up like a corpse ready to be frozen. Other times the golden glow that emanated from her skin reminded one of fantasies on the beach, fantasies that were finally coming true.

She was all bottled up with a special kind of stress she only got when she went back to New York to visit her folks. The city's creepy emotional violence had suffocated her and the sense of anonymity she had walking the big avenues filled her with so many questions (philosophical) that she would generate more potential juice (to explode) than she knew what to do with. Her special brand of bitch-castration-philosophy building up inside her resulted in a magic juice whose promise to come out all sweet and stringy was always on my mind. I had never encountered anything like it. And I was sure it had to do with what she was thinking (and maybe a little genetic manipulation: she came from a very wealthy family: her father was a world renown bio-engineer). The other thing that built up her potential explosions was dope.

Shapiro smoked a lot of dope. In New York especially. She needed it. She needed it just to get by. She couldn't spend twelve hours in the city without either calling a contact (most of which were disappearing) or, if really desperate, going to Washington Square Park to pick up a small bag of black ice. The dope circulated her sexual self in the form of poisoned blood that fed all the discrete parts of her psyche which hid inside millions of tiny places all covered up by her designer jeans body. She only wore tight jeans because she knew they made her slightly big ass thoroughly enticing. There were times when I would just lean over her and start gnawing on the raw cotton fanny forgetting the rest of her.

Until I could take it no more and would have a helluva time trying to take them off (she usually helped) so that I could go for the cheese (she had no idea that her ejaculations were the rarest form of nutrience ever produced by a human product and only when I informed her of this did she start getting uppity about it and often threatened an all-out cunt-sanction unless I did things for her).

We spent a lot of time talking philosophy. In my attempts to fictionalize its essentiality, she became ferociously opposed to everything about me but in the end admitted that it only made her crave me that much more. I felt as if I were on to something.

*

When she got back from New York she had decided that my dentist wasn't good enough for her. She felt that despite the fact he would probably be good with kids, there was still the problem of genetics, the kind of kids he would help reproduce. She said something about "one anal-retentive parent would be more than enough." She wanted more than she thought he could offer. I wasn't necessarily "more" but I would do until she ran into someone else who could be a father for her children. Someone who really knew how to procreate and had The Right Stuff. Until then she would concentrate on being a trust-fund pseudo-bohemian poetess/workaholic who needed to continuously come. I could help make her come. For some odd reason I felt obliged.

She came into the condo an hour and a half later than expected. I was cranking on a compilation tape of Stereolab, Meat Puppets, Pavement and Mazzy Star. I was stoned out of my mind. Some good stuff had reappeared on the market and a friend of mine had thrown a bit my way. I was horny.

Shapiro immediately took her tight jeans off (something of a chore to be sure) and was walking over to me with a look of startled passion on her strangely contorted face. It was as if she had never seen me before and was surprised that I was sitting on *her* floor (leaning against the couch) not paying much attention to her big beautiful ass and encroaching twat. I was too stoned to try and figure her out.

She moved onto me with one continuous movement straddling my body.

"Fuck me. Make me come."

Her hand was rubbing my sweat pants along the inside of my upper legs and my cock got hard. I was horny and responsive. She was hot and ready to explode all that potent stress juice she accumulated in the Big Apple.

"I need you so bad my mind won't even stop me from feeling good about you. Just the thought...just the *thought* of you fucking me..."

Philosophy on the brink. Forget implosion. Shapiro was not just another TV junky letting imagination slip to the back burner. She was Northeast Jewish Pussy that, despite troubled times and insistent consensual culture pressuring her to emerge stringently homogeneous without anything *remotely* resembling a radical self, despite it all, found herself philosophically situated in the right place at the right time: all aboard my anarchic ship of perverse sexuality rubbing itself up against an iceberg of tenuous infrastructure.

Two hours before her arrival I had just finished working out in the gym. I had enslaved myself to forty minutes of high-speed Stairmaster. I was a glandular mess. I could've easily showered but that would've spoiled the welcome home party that I knew she would want to get into just as soon as she could get her tight-ass jeans off. This was my way of telling her I still wanted her.

The more you get to know someone the more you can expect them to act certain ways. Every lover's expectations are steeped in the Other's knowledge of what it is *they* need. Love, or so I'm learning, is a game of knowledge and intuition. It's up to each player to participate according to the rules of *need*. I knew Shapiro needed me, but I knew much more than that, for instance, I was very well aware of the fact that she had this thing for me when I smelled especially badly and sure enough she had no problem dealing with it this time as she snuffed me out killing all the bacteria in a series of licks and feels and somnambulistic sucks that made me almost think she could become some kind of seriously fun love-artist.

She reached out and grabbed my enormously excited cock, grabbed it so it kind of hurt. She had a knack for applying just enough pressure to cause pain but not so much that I instinctively felt the need to strike back. Her long red fingernail was poking around the throbbing blue head just barely scratching the surface.

Shapiro looked at me like she would easily ruin me. There wasn't the least bit of caution floating in her sanguine eyes. She gave me a kooky almost maddening look like she was going to destroy me. Her red fingernail gently tapped at the bloody head of all my confusion. I thought I was a goner.

She took the cock in her mouth and started slurping it with her big driveling tongue. Her eyes were looking deep inside my own and as soon as I thought to myself how good it would be if she took her free hand and played with my balls that's just what she did.

94

She was taking me inside her oozing cunt. On top of me she started gyrating to a self-imposed rhythm. Her smirk indicated that the feeling was alright. Instead of seeing a wide array of potential Others to drip my spermy dreams into, I ended up losing interest in what was happening and opened my eyes becoming somewhat stoic in my performance. But her eyes were closed and she was fucking somebody really good. She seemed to be eluding herself. Drooling spit and smirk. Then some moaning and finally a long loud *Ugghh* that was accompanied by an ejaculation of that special Shapiro cumjuice (the contents of which will never be revealed). She fell back onto the floor and passed out.

All I know is that despite my disinterest in her at that particular point in time, I still found myself craving the groovy gravy shit she just spilled all over our dead sex organs. So I took some off my dick and started eating it. Shapiro, wild Sabra Sister, was a big wet blob of rich cunt. Curled up on the floor. She was home again....

SUCKING ON THE BLACK BOSOM
THAT IS MY BODY

But who is this? Who is this that dares to drag the annular segments of its body over my black bosom? Whoever you are, realize that your total lack of pretext does not excuse your ridiculous presence. How long do you suppose it will take for you too to take on the image of the ultimate carcinogenic nightmare impostering a human being? Suck on me long enough and the highly resinated bongwater with its syrupy chemical glue that slowly drips out of my time-worn nipple and into your mouth will have its desired effect: you will feel at once purposive and maddened with lust; you will crave for gardens of youthful genitalia as it grows out of the forests of innocent flesh begging for contact with your criminal consciousness. Spilling yourself out in load after load of seminal discharge you will single-handedly create an entire new generation of sexually literate readers!

Listen to me: never forget that if your sumptuous brain has believed me capable of offering you a few words of consolation, it could only be the motive of an ignorance totally devoid of physiognomical knowledge. Can't you see that you're coming face-to-face with the last moral truth to resound on this dead planet? Isn't time you recognized the murderous indifference that splays itself here in the hum of a neutered glory? This is the streamlined sterility of a useless composition, the radical impotence that consciously seeks to deprive you of "connectivity".

But this is what you need, isn't it? Can't you see that

"connectivity" falsifies experience? Yet you still wish to see it all come together for purposes of what you call moral relief. How self-effacing! Instead of accepting the challenge of exploding fragments that burst into a multitude of unrecognizable and even further disconnected fragments, you beg for cohesion, the chance to neatly wrap all your gifts with the same dull paper, each gift perfectly wrapped and put inside a box larger than itself, this process continuing non-stop until all you have left is a world gift-wrapped in a box big enough to contain the world. And yet despite this gnawing sensation that tears at your heart and implores you to generate an entirely different perspective, you have the nerve to sheepishly look this ultimate gift-horse in the mouth! Well, okay, if you must deceive yourself then you'll get what you deserve, but before you sink into the final death of a rigged complacency, take a good look at this gift-horse you're having difficulty handling: notice that the gums are bleeding, the reins have come undone, the bridle is shooting laser beams into your eyes! Eyes that can't distinguish between a ruthless ideology out to dismantle your sense of feeling and a truly beautiful celestial vision!

But already this seems to want to regiment itself in the perversion of binary oppositions that unthinkingly seem destined to keep the ruthless ideology alive in its killing glee! The problem with this is that binary oppositions no longer have a bite on the real. We now know this to be the case. The real has become a distant simulation of itself so that you can't recognize the *difference* anymore. *Difference* has lost itself in the quest for future "connectivity" but what a waste! I can already feel the nerve of raw energy transplant a strange paradise in my soul which is blacker than the sky you live under! It takes me no time at all to see that my newfound trade of Profound Desiring has created a concomitant flow that no longer belongs to "either/or" but constitutes the asymmetrical becoming of the two! I am not Man! I am not Woman! I am the residue of machines making love! This thick molasses that composes my dream of Being crawls over everything living and breathing and smothers it to death only to contract itself with a heretofore unheard of strength that crushes the futile human flesh into piles of broken glass! Then one final squeeze of my viscous body and the glass remnants of all the ages becomes pulverized into the finest grains of sand ever created by any God in any metaphysical solar system to date! Oceans of lust come in waves of despair and hopelessness washing into the desert of my soul and moistens its essence until there's nothing left but brimming fluidity! My life!

Let me repeat: the end of the world is ONE HUMAN wandering the desert of his own soul until the great sea of corruption and perversity pounds through his heart and dilutes his spirit in such an efficient manner that he (the last vestige of conscious life on earth) *becomes* the final moment. This final moment will be the much spoken end of history. When there is no more history there is no more grass. When there is no more grass you will have learned your moral lesson. The moral lesson will have been that beauty can no longer exist in this world we once inhabited. The idea of a world and its beauty will have become absolutely impossible...

CRASHPAD

Hormone calmly collects herself and smiles. I'm at the other end of the table.

All of the tables are community tables in that anybody who's eating at the Soup Kitchen is allowed to eat with anybody else. Those are the rules. So if you want privacy or hate the company of arbitrary human beings then this is not the place for you.

The Soup Kitchen is last resort food substance for walking zombies who are nothing but the gristle of a social war machine that sets many different energies against each other and forces the Cantor of Tales to recut his or her personal collage of piecemeal existence. The dirt and grime of street life is so thick and imprinted on the skin of any potential feeling that you can't even call the thing that writes these words sentient.

Institutional noise infiltrates all partially-clogged port-holes that halfheartedly resist entry into the body. Food substance rumbles a talk consistent with the language of ulcers. Enzymes try to reorganize the mismanaged mucus walls. Internal lacerations cut into the equation. The problematics of need are schizophrenic and make the body divisive. This body could be anybody's but relays itself to the surrounding world as something in particular named Hormone. Hormone keeps smiling. She wants to fuck. She always wants to fuck.

She's got a platinum-blond mohawk turquoise eyes and is

missing a few teeth. She talks to the slob next to her: "My parents never bought me braces because my sister was dyslexic and they only had x amount of money to spend on their children. Since I was smart and could have been a lawyer or a doctor, they gave my sister Hanna all the money to learn how to read and spell and shit like that. Now I'm starving and Hanna is head bagboy at Kroger's. Figures, eh?"

I smile back. I used to fuck Hormone when we both lived near the creek, in a cave.

She winks at me and licks her lips. Her nose twitches. Eyes fluttering. She's still got it despite all the grime.

I see her put her hand under the table as she looks at me like she's getting off (masturbating). I keep eating my kidney bean soup watching her face turn colors. She's a great actress. She really knows how to be a show-off.

Eventually she pulls her hand out from underneath the table and there's a tiny glob of whitish yellow muck on the end of her finger. No telling what it is. It could be anything (a new strain of slut bacteria). She sucks it off like candy.

*

I follow her out of the Kitchen and out into the cold.
She's holding my hand.

Hand holding with Hormone provokes a kind of *narcosis*. Her touch benumbs my crucial sensibilities as I flounder for meaningful discourse. Now that I'm playing it straight and have a real gig with time off for sickness I feel like I've betrayed her. We used to ceremonially smear blood in each others faces to form a bond against the world that rich creeps were rhetorically calling Humanity. And now I was on a pension plan. I felt like a total shit.

"I'm still fluid. My feeling is that I could love you if you'd let me."

She assures me it's not possible. She says, "Love's a priori, something somebody *feels*, and I don't feel, besides, I'm too good for you." She lets go of my hand and starts walking faster. I still follow her.

Back at her tiny louse pad I tell her I think I still love her. What else could this feeling rumbling inside my gut be? It's so *alive* I almost want to write a poem or something. I used to write poems for her. There used to be plenty of time for everything.

She takes off her t-shirt and jeans. She's been barefoot ever since I met her. She doesn't *believe* in shoes. Even when it's below freezing. Most of her toes are permanently blackblue. The bottom of her feet are scummy from the polluted city streets. The taste of metallic grit reentrenches itself in my memory as I flashback to the last time I sucked her feet in horrid deprecation of my useless self.

Now I had a gig and was bringing home a steady paycheck. I was beyond the scum. And yet I had taken on a worst odor, the odor of a maleficent slave-wage worker. It was the most corrupt vapor any human meat ever exuded. I couldn't stop the mad rumble of queasy feelings from displacing my jumbled priorities. I wanted to pretend that I didn't love her.

She put a Pere Ubu cassette into her battered beatbox. It all made sense in a way that chilled me.

"I can't keep this up. I've really gotta go. I'm sorry I wasted your time."

*

"Do you wanna hear some poetry I just wrote this morning?

101

You'll love it, I'm sure. It'll remind you of the old days."

I really had no choice. Her poetry put a spell on me and I liked the way I felt when I was under her spell. So I just sat on the one chair she had in her room and waited for her to get the poetry.

She had a tough time finding it in the midst of all the trash that grew in piles all around her miniscule living space. When she finally found it (it was written on a brown grocery bag) she laid on the floor in front of me and propped her feet up onto my lap. They smelled terrible but I started rubbing them nonetheless. It was as if I was addicted to some unknown agent whose microscopic tumors of lust had enveloped my decayed brain.

"Okay," she began, "let's see, oh yeah, I call it 'Mortal's Malady'":

> ostracized, a headache with a beauty
> mark tracing my face through the dead
> of memory manifesting a rear-guard
> raunch of haunches spilling bloody
> freak meat, I Am A Light Fixture
> waiting to be turned on. These
> bulbous pustules that grow on
> my decrepit skin are the bubbles
> of pleasure I bathe in. I no longer
> want this body but have decided
> that it needs to become the same
> social killing machine that Others
> fuck *me* with. Therefore I am:
>
> custard coming in nonstop
> repetitive discharging
> ON YOUR COCK
> *you need me*

and she quickly got up off the floor and started swatting me with the grocery bag as hard she could. She was crying her eyes out.

I asked her if we could go to her bed and sleep. She agreed that it was probably the best thing to do and I fell asleep with my chin on her shoulder.

*

When I awoke, Hormone was looking down at me stroking my hair. She said: "You know, all human beings use other human beings for their enjoyment. For their own advancement and pleasure. It's a known fact and the more someone says 'you just use me' or after the fucking has ended 'you just used me' I always smile and say that yes I know but that's what humans do. I know it better than anybody. I enjoy using and being used. It's the basis of all value. There's really nothing like it."

She slid herself down the bed and started blowing me. I started eating her. This was where we had left off the last time. Mutual supplication.

As I was eating her I imagined I was calling her on the phone and telling her to expect me in five minutes. When I got off work I wanted to come to her shithole and walk right in. The door had to be unlocked. When I entered her crashpad I wanted her to crawl over to me totally naked and take off my boots. Then I wanted her to climb up my legs and strip me of my pants. Then I wanted her to suck me and swallow all my come. Most importantly, I wanted her to make sure that she never looked at me in the eyes during the whole scene. And after she sucked me off and swallowed me whole I wanted her to turn her body around and crawl back to her bed until I left. I wanted her to be completely silent, not a word. No eye contact. Ever again.

Then I would hang up the phone.

About five minutes later I would enter through the unlocked front door and I would see her crawl over to me with her head looking down on the ground whereupon she would kiss my leather snowboot. She would spend an inconsiderable amount of time licking and kissing my boots. I wanted the whole experience to be silent and I wouldn't stand for this ridiculous boot-licking.

"I'm not a fucking *machine*," I would tell her, "I don't need you to slobber over the equipment. I need you to suck me. Obey the flesh that tells you what to do, not the product that coats it."

Looking down at the floor, she would speak in a low whisper: "*You're* the product that coats it. *You're* the leather boot. You're ingrained in my mind as nothing but hide. There's nothing inside of you because I'm your inside and I'm outside. That's the reality you don't want to deal with but have to deal with. Right now you're nothing but dead leather. I'm licking you for my own satisfaction. I like the taste of leather. It's all that's left of you. It's the only thing I really dig about you."

I would swat her across the side of the head. I would hear her ear pop and the ringing in her head would cause her instant vertigo. At that point she would change into something way out of my control.

"Good," she would say, "*hit* me, beat the shit out of me, hit me Big Man, I can't *come* unless Big Man hits the shit out of me, *hit me* Big Man…" and then she would start licking the boot ferociously.

Looking into the leather boots, in between licks, she

would keep saying (girllike), "Hit me love, I really *do* love the way you hit me…"

Of course I wouldn't hit her. The only reason I could imagine it the one time (the only time I would ever imagine hitting a woman) was because my dream of maximum control was falling apart on me just when I thought I had finally succeeded at something. What a joke. She was looking up at me.

I slugged her in the face with my pummeling fist.

It knocked her back. She was leaning back on her hands with her legs spread wide. She flapped her legs like wings (half nervously / half intimidating me). Her nose was a bruised rose bleeding.

She said, blood pouring into her mouth, unable to stop it, "I promise not to look at you. I'll never say another word to you again. I'll totally cease to exist for you, that's how strong my love is. Not a word, ever, really, because that would be…"

She was looking right at me.

I wanted to leave and teach her a lesson. But I couldn't. I was weak. I was human I was weak. I was human I wasn't even human I was just plain fucking weak. Not even human I crawled across the floor to her outstretched legs and came up to her bloody face to kiss her with passionate frenzy and she came across with a hard right fist just below my left eye and it really hurt. I felt my eye swell with the pain of hard emotions. I was crying.

"Good," she said, "very good, very *very* good, Big *Big* Man, my forever and ever daddy lover. We're gonna have kids and a house and a car and more kids. Imagine *that*…."

SOCIAL DARWINISM

Walking down the street looking for something disease-free and ready to give itself over to me I came across a half-insect half-human creature that spent all its "waking" hours taking deep carb hits of black ice. Black ice was concentrated lung-matter ripped out of the bodies of disease-free crack addicts most of whom were baby-whores who fell into the wrong hands. These corpse's lungs were processed with various other substances, particularly crack, and remolded into little rock fragments that kind of looked like black hash. Contrary to most smokables, this shit had a horrid odor and when it burned smelled like a minor holocaust. The half-insect half-human creature smoking the shit was curled up into a wall underneath a Lox Stock & Bagel bakery sign. This wasn't the disease-free blowjob-intense comrade I was hoping to find but maybe it could help me locate what I was after.

"You fuckhead," the viral thing said to me, "don't you know who I am?"

The closer I got to it the more I realized it was one of the guys I used to work with when I first came to the city some fifteen years earlier. He had gotten "The Bug". "The Bug" was the most dangerous strain of T.B. to ever find its way into the body. His features were so grimy and gruesome, his face so grotesquely distorted, that it was hardly him. His cough sounded like the call of death itself. His Cuban accent was still with him as was his conservative Republican ideology.

106

Despite what had happened to him.

"Laz," I said, "you look terrible man."

"Fuck you *pinga*," he flicked his bic and took another hit off the carb but it was empty.

"Here," I said, "take this...plug it in your box." I had handed him a DAT tape full of Instant Karma, the hardcore variety. It was known to relieve the brutal tension caused by the "The Bug".

"Oh please. No more punk shit. I can't take."

"But you must. This is the only thing that's gonna help clear your head."

"Por favor, shithead, this is no-thing. No one will want to listen to this to survive. To hear shit is not hearing."

"C'mon Laz, this stuff works and you know it. Motherfuckers keep dissing you and all you can do is suck up their shit. It's crazy, Man, and you know it."

"Yeah yeah. Crazy. You making a no good sense you-self you fucking *pinga*. It never seem right, this headache shit. Nothing help it. You can play program all day long and I no get better. Why not you leave me be to my-self. I can die my own way. Too many other thing to worry bout than you and this punk-rave shit."

"But the cause of this worrying, the fury behind your eyes, Laz, I can see it. They fucked you up good."

"No no. You no see fury. I fucked *my-self* up goo'. I had big chance to make monee. I had monee amigo. I had big monee. Now I'm Bug. Bug has me fucked up. No choice. This Amerika." He kept shaking his head and coughing.

"You've got to break down the negative flow. Don't get caught up in it. It's not good for you. Come with me: I'll give you the cure."

"You no know what good for me. I'm happy clown

working death machine every day. And happy to do it too."

It was obvious that he still thought he had a job. "The Bug" was so strong that he would just get lost in the reel-time of past experience although the fact of the matter is that he got canned as soon as the Boss caught him stealing from the petty cash fund to help support his ice-habit.

"Got no other thing to do but work big dead thing until I bleed to death my-self which is what I do best," he went on not thinking but rattling, shaking, coughing, vocally contorting: "This why I funny about you ugly death punk shit. It no make sense. You think cunt and cock and pussy shit go goo' wid me? I tell you something. You don know shit. Big monee death machine has bigger dick than you ever dream. It make big cum job work miracles on your head. You think you different but deep inside you same monee person. You got it made."

He was still spewing his conservative rationalizations to me like he was caught in the heat of a gospel. Reagan had been dead for eight years.

"I'm not sure I understand, Laz, maybe..."

"Naw, motherfuck, you no unnerstan shit. You go fuck word shit and then come out like big-time talker bullshit. I can see now. You say you know everything but shit fly out your head like you have no control. You think control be bad shit but I know you better than you know you. Real control shit is in your head. It no outside. Outside is nothing. Not even a goddam problem for me."

"But Laz, the way you get treated Man, you must admit, sometimes it really pisses you off...."

"Yeah yeah I get pissed off. I get pissed off at asshole like you making my life miserable shit I can't even be happy. I'm happiest motherfucker alive. I swim in big pool of happiness.

My whole life one big ocean of happiness with bullshit sharks like you eating my head off. I wanna watch TV. Okay?"

"Okay. But I'm going to watch it with you." I watched him pull out from his coat pocket a very old portable 4-inch Sony Watchman. He played with the tuner and volume until he got a daytime talk-show where they were talking to divorced parents of serial killers. I crouched over his shoulder making sure not to rub my skin on his open scabs.

"No good you watch TV wid me. You talk shit wid TV. TV make more sense than you wid your shit when you talk TV. I no unnerstan you TV talk. What you mean?"

"What do *you* mean? I didn't say anything..."

"I mean what you mean when you talk you TV shit. You always got big commercial problem hanging out your butt. You no like to buy shit?"

He was still caught up in some bad reel-time.

"SHIT MAN! You no make no good sense to me. You say you Amerikan. You say you love country. You say you tired of shit but then you don go out and buy shit. What you work for?"

"Good question. I'm not sure..."

"No man, you not sure of no shit. I think you better off dead. You can't live for nothing. You gotta have shit to do, to buy shit. Ain't no way man. Now lemme watch TV. And you can't watch it wid me. You go do some stupid rave shit. That all you goo for."

I got up and decided to check out The Strip. As soon as I got onto Broadway a girl asked me if I wanted a blowjob for three dollars. I told her that I was looking for some CLEAN and she said she was and could prove it.

I took this to mean that we could go drop in Doctor Veblen's office and she nodded. She couldn't have been more than 12 or 13. She was wearing a black leather skirt, an

Esprit green-silk shirt and Nike crosstrainers. She carried an old stuffed animal with her: A Mutant Ninja Turtle.

Off 49th Street upstairs on the third floor of a building that on the ground floor was a sex show complete with Bug-infested derelicts and chromosome-injected baby whores was Doctor Veblen's office. The floor had sawdust on it and the doctor, behind a desk with his back toward us, was concentrating on a big computer screen that seemed connected to a coffin-shaped table that had a glass bubble over it.

"Hello," I said.

He turned around and looked up at us. He seemed to show chagrin.

"What do you need?" he asked.

"She says she's CLEAN. I'm just making sure."

"She's CLEAN," he said and leaned back into his chair kicking his feet up onto his desk. "She was just in here yesterday. Everything checks out okay."

"I guess you ran a ..."

Veblen kicked his feet down and leaned forward, slightly agitated.

"A Round-The-World, yes, a complete infrared imaging with bone scanning and blood testing; the works." He spoke in complete deadpan indifference: "We even went up the anus. I have the documentation if you'd like to see it."

As soon as he said anus, the girl, sucking her thumb and holding her Mutant Turtle tight against her chest, contorted and groaned. I looked in her eyes and saw she was in reel-time.

I still needed to make sure. Bad lungs weren't worth anything on the black market and I needed her lungs worse than I needed her mouth or cunt.

"TB?" I asked.

"Negative," he assured me.

"VD 90?"

"Negative. None of the VD's."

"AIDS?"

"Negative, nothing, nothing at all, except maybe a little *habit*..." he winked at me as if he knew my game and I just nodded back at him not really interested in his pseudo-camaraderie.

I told him I didn't need to see the documentation and thanked him. His was actually a government service but I still offered him a few bucks. He declined, saying they were worthless to him and that I should save them for the baby-whores who survived on them. I put my arm around the girl and took her to my hotel on 47th where I was staying on the eleventh floor. Inside the room it was easy to get her to undress but she didn't want to let go of Stuffy, her mutant friend.

"Don't worry, Stuffy'll be alright. We can play with him later. Right now I want you to be a big girl and give me the blowjob you promised."

"Okay," she said, real easy now that I had unbuttoned my Levi's and pulled out the full fourteen inches. It was bobbing around dying for a suck.

She went for it but I stopped her. "Wait," I said, "I have a better idea."

I lifted her up off the ground and put her over my shoulder then in one swift movement grabbed her ankles and swung her back around me so that now I held onto her ankles above my head. She was hanging there so that her face was now rubbing against my huge cock. I told her my strength could only hold her like this for so long and that she had to work fast. She didn't say anything but started breathing heavy licking and slurping and kissing and generally eating it.

"You're gonna have to jerk your whole head, your entire body, to get that good throat rhythm going. Grab my ass."

She caught on real quick and was soon gobbling the huge shaft which must have penetrated deep inside her past the esophagus in toward the lungs. Her little girl lubricant was the unctuous fluid cannibals dreamed of and the slick motoricity of her whole head creating a momentum all to its own was enough to make my balls explode with unrelenting joy and cream-filled derision!

She choked on the sheer amount of it all and holding her even higher I could see the sperm drip out of her mouth right onto the floor. She was heaving and grunting like she had never swallowed so much come in all her young life and I thought it was important for her to have every last drop so I lowered her toward the floor whereupon I asked her if she would please use her tongue and lick up what she had inconsiderately allowed to leak on the floor. Like a good three-dollar baby-whore she did as I asked and when it was all off the floor I slowly dropped her whole body to the floor where she promptly crumpled into a ball of insignificant nothingness and crashed out. Apparently an overdose of sinking blood had rocked her head in a dizzying heatwarp and she'd probably be out for a good while. I wasn't sure how long I wanted to keep her but in the meantime had time to read and write and wash myself as well as catch a meal on The Strip.

When I came back to my room she was up and at the desk reading.

"Hi Honey," I said, "I'm home."

She looked up from her book.

112

"Hey, sweety," she said. "Where have you been? I was worried about you?"

"Oh, I just grabbed a bite to eat. Falafels and french-fries. What are you reading?"

"Oh, nothing special." She put the book down and stood up.

"What's up?" I asked.

"Well, for starters, I threw Stuffy away. Right out the window." She laughed.

"Uh-huh. And now what will you do?"

"I'll be yours, to have and to hold and to protect."

"But I don't want to *have* anything. Besides, there *is* no protection anymore. We are holding our own, so to speak, in a holding pattern, soon to be wedded with our godforsaken reality, a permanent crash-site. It's like, dead, baby, honestly truly sincerely dead."

"You're so negative, like, why the rush? We just got started."

"I'm not rushing things here. You're the one talking about..."

"You could make good money off me. I'm CLEAN. Is that a problem for you or do you *prefer* to die young?"

"Who's talking about dying?"

"I thought *you* were. Listen: I will do whatever you want me to..." the sound of her words echoed in her mind and she said them aloud, again: "I will do whatever you want..."

"What I want is to dispose of you. You need not live anymore. Believe me, it's not worth it. Are you a crack addict?"

"Yes. I was hoping you had some...."

"I know. That's why you need me. That's why *everybody* needs me. But listen: you can make me a lot of money, it's

113

true, although not by giving three-dollar baby-whore blowjobs. That shit just don't fly anymore. I need big money. Real big. Without the big money coming in regular-like, I'll end up catching 'The Bug' and then that's it, I'm a goner."

"What about that raving punk shit, those tapes. Can't you make some of them? I heard they..."

"All the punk and rave shit does is keep you from going over the edge, but, hanging on the edge perpetually looking down at how far you're gonna fall, what's the use? It's really simple: I don't want to see myself get to that point. So, what I need from you is your life, your body. C'mon, I'm taking you to Oleander Mill."

And I grabbed her by the arm, led her out of the hotel, hailed a cab and took off for the northernmost part of the city. It was there that Oleander Mill poisoned her with an overdose of black ice. He forced her to take too many carb hits and eventually it suffocated her brain and she was gone. This enabled Mill to cut into her chest and get her lungs which, after thorough re-testing, he then processed with a bunch of other stuff particularly crack and leftover black ice powder. Mill's test results were the same as Veblen's: he said she was CLEAN, only the habit, which in this case, would actually make the processed lung-shit even stronger than it already was. This was the most highly concentrated drug residue ever created. Mill and I split up the goods evenly. I had close to ten pounds of it. This would assure my survival for at least another year.

I took the shit back to my room and went to my desk where I opened my diary and wrote:

> *We can judge of the beauty of life only by that of death. We can love with all our hearts those in whom*

114

we recognize great faults. Despair is the least of our errors. We are not content with the life we have within us. We wish to live the ideas of others, in an imaginary life. We force ourselves to appear as we are. We labor to preserve this imaginary being, which is none other than the real. But how can I even begin to alter my perception of the real when, without warning, the death machination of corporate-sponsored reel-time invades my very own solitude? And why does this solitude consist of a multi-dimensionality so powerful in its ability to arbitrarily change course depending on the mood of the navigator? It seems that nothing is less strange than these contradictions I constantly find myself absorbed in. There can be no doubt that we cretins, who destroy the environment with our chemically-altered culture, are in no position to judge the beauty of anything, not even life, for we have found comfort and relief in the palace of death....

I WANT MY MTV

He's an absolutely naked woman on stage speaking into a microphone asking the audience of some fifty patrons as many questions as he can get out of his system:

Do you wanna fuck me?

What are we having for dinner?

Do you wanna suck me off?

Who's that woman he's with?

Do you wanna stick your finger up my asshole?

How many times have I told you to please stop saying that about me?

Do you wanna stick your tongue in my ear and be a human q-tip?

Are you willing to go that far with him?

116

Do you wanna drink my urine and spread my shit on your tits only to let me cut off your nipples and plug your nose up with them?

Did he promise you anything?

Do you wanna shit in my face and ram the sharp PVC pipe up my ass while whispering how much you love me?

Where did she go?

Do you wanna buy that young girl on the corner of 47th and Broadway who just asked you if you wanna date?

In what way do I remind you of him? Is he still alive? When did he do those things to you?

Do you wanna buy her and take her back to your chic apartment on Central Park West and tie her up to your bed and feed her nothing but sperm and human excrement for three weeks straight until

Have you heard the news?

117

she dies of starvation and malnutrition and bloody beatings to the head?

Why bother?

Do you wanna go into work and call your secretary into the office only to have her lock the door so you can pull out your cock and gun demanding that she suck you off & after you come in her mouth pull the trigger and blow her skull away?

If you want to do it that way then I guess we'll do it that way, but do you *really* want to?

Do you write every day?

What does your mom think about all of this?

Does this sound like FUN?

Do you wanna fuck?

118

THERAPY

OR,

THE REVOLUTION OF EVERYDAY LIFE

I told you; no works, no language, no words,

no mind, nothing. Nothing, except fine

Nerve-Scales. A sort of impenetrable stop

in the midst of everything in our minds.

—Artaud

Wakes up in the morning no papamummy continuously regurgitating open wounds of indifference. Eyes smothered in a dense fog the precipitation of no memory crawling out of the ocean onto the shore reeling in nextphase transformation circumventing new bug mentality always in the process of recovering random self-identity perpetually on trial a revolution of poetic happenstance dancing trance-like in polymorphically perverse mindless walking through the village back toward the apartment where an easy going happy nonchalant pyrotechnics of sensual wonder awaits.

Living in a $6-a-night apartment in Lagos Portugal turning tricks just for the fuck of it. An odd affiliation with love sex money power diatribe soul-searching etc. Consciously turning recently excavated hard body into somebody else's bad habit. Fully rehabilitated ready to send dreamworthy streams of concomitant cum into the upper vulva regions of as many women as he possibly can. Politically shooting himself in unincorporated free enterprise zones without seeming the most incorrect application of spiritual energy possible. Still Mal. Always Mal. Maybe a recharged idiosyncratic internally transmogrified Mal but still deep down inside the same: a human being: gender type: Male.

Writing his chants in the overdetermined womb of infrastructural decay hadn't produced a new awareness as planned. Just more lust. More craving. More desire to penetrate. The tip of his dyseased marker floating around the magic writing pad looking for action. Traversing the village like a roaming hoarding dangerous spiritually reconstructed reignited Malediction. Mal: the curse of language erupting.

*

Mal told Angela, who had spent the night at his pad, that he was going into town to buy some fresh goat cheese. On his way down the side street where the small shop that carried the cheese hid in a recess that guaranteed no *touristas*, Mal ran into a live wetdream that hit him like a tidal wave of emotion-filled memory. The live wetdream was a highly intelligent well-stocked American machine made of beauty warmth concentrated love and exotica. Her name was Janet Jackson and she was African-American. The last time he had seen her, in Soho, she had just changed her name to Zulu Red Earth.

"Hey Mal!"

"Zoo. I haven't seen you since..."

"Yeah, I know, tell me about it."

They hugged and Mal felt his toned tanned body melt in her powerful grip.

"But what are you doing here? I mean I came to get *away* from all my...not that I'm not happy to see you, I'm just..."

"Shocked. You just got tidal waved, didn't ya? That's cool. You know it's meant to be Baby. Meant...to...be.... This isn't just coincidence. It's more than that. It's...synchronicity. I guess we're just stuck in some parallel ghost-rhythm or something. Better than being fellow slave-zombies back in the States, eh Mal? Speaking of which, lemme tell you man, I had a hard time back home. The States suck big dick amigo. You dig? It's like...well, you know the score just as well as I do. Same old same old: great times in college followed by immediate entry into the real-time real-world bullshit of corporate America and its suck-you-dry program of take-take-take until you got no more to give, Full

121

Bodymind Takeover Energy, the universal credit line (I owe
k / you owe *k*), *then*, by the time you realize something
personal and worthwhile might be out there to latch onto,
something akin to love or whatever it is we vagrant college
graduates with nothing to look forward to go after in our
iddy-biddy social world of too-much-fake-reality, nothing
substantial comes of it, no real interpersonal relationship to
work on cause Big Daddy Corporation and his rhetoric-
programmed automatons in Washington already got your
and his time earmarked for other important operations like
pushing fiber optic keyboard referendums on the poor who,
it turns out, *you are*, what makes you be the thing you is, dig?,
cause I'm *already* fried of that shit and am only 28. 28 Mal.
And I was already cranking out 50-plus hours a week saying
bye-bye to me-oh-my. That shit's just plain old bullshit. NOT
ME. So I cashed in my retirement fund, took the penalty,
hung with the folks for a few months tellin' 'em about my
transfers, put-downs, dis- and relocations, whatever, and
they were sweet and tried to understand but in the end found
it hard NOT to try and get me motivated to go back into it all
again. See, they got theirs, and so they still got faith even
though the facts are pointing in a different direction. They
don't see that I'm not stabilizing on account of their and
their generation's total lack of concern for what my generation is growing into which is a big heaping smelly steaming
pile of dogshit with a McDonalds napkin smushed on top it.
Dig?"

"Sure, I dig. I'm always diggin on you, Zoo. It's amazing.
Here I am in the only get-away zone left and here you are too.
It's incredible. You're the same far-away planet I always
wanted to transport my ratty-ass self to. You're an alien love
connection. People on earth have no idea what it's like any-

122

more. You're so far-out, baby, like E.T. but with the all the *nice*."

"You see Mal, it's like this: Ain't shit worth depending on. Buying into the shit ain't worth it. No-fucking-body's got any kind of future with these fuckheads runnin' the joint. I'm really pissed Man. But at least here, in the sun and away from the gun, I'm happy. Having some fun. I can groove on this scene for as long my money holds. And when it's gone then maybe I'll be gone or those fuckheads tryin' to bullshit me'll be gone. Bottom line is that for the most part I'm homeless, dig? Homeless. Even when I had that jerky-ass corporate gig sharing some high-rise with a rich white cunt who had the folks sendin' in some extra to help smooth everything out around the edges, I was homeless. I said to myself, Zoo baby, Homey is where your shit is. Your damn heart. And you know something Mal, it really is."

She looked so fine, so connected. Her long black dreads were hanging all over. Every time she paused in her diatribe she smiled at me like she was still in love with me which I imagined she was. Her feet were huge yet smooth as if made of the rarest ebony available to man. Toenails painted darkred exposed in the full sunlight. Sandals so thin you could say she was barefoot. Barefoot and pregnant with the thought of terrorizing the phony white world!

"So what are you doing?"

"Me?"

"No Mal, the ghost you're playing. What's *he* doing?!"

"Oh *him*! Well, he's all lost in wonder and approach, as usual. Only so much beauty he can stand. I mean, in a little woman, especially a little white woman, he can turn on and absorb all that's there. An appetizer. But *you* Zoo, you're like a big black wet dream drenching me in so much thick weather that I'm about to crash. System's overloading.

123

Cockpit's steaming. Could throttle my whole lifestory right into *you*. That strong, baby. That powerful. That beautiful."

She just smiles her teeth stretch out to the sea. Her thick pink tongue curls at the end, some promiscuous star-creature that sucks up your jellyfish balls in one fell swoop. The smell of roasted *coffea arabica* emanates from her skin.

"You wanna get some coffee?"

"Well, I do, but, uh, you see, I've gotta, well, it's just..."

"You're cool. Don't explain it baby; just keep mumbling. I get the picture. Mal's got him some foreign sugar exchange goin' on. Making it up as you go along, right? As always. Don't freak. I'll get mine. You and me got some catching up to do anyway. Shit, I could *be* here for awhile. Right now I'm over at the Rubi Mar. Room 11. All by my lonesome."

"Lonesome," Mal repeated to himself. She was playing off his weaknesses.

She gave Mal a long wet kiss right in the middle of the skinny alley not stopping for anything not even the crazy zigzagging bicyclist with the big box of newspapers strapped onto to his back rack. As she filled Mal's mouth with her long salty tongue fishing for more intensity by way of total togetherness, she grabbed hold of his hard skinny ass just like in his dreams. She was the literal translation of the term Man-Handler. She was the Great Mother Earth. The Every Only Love Goddess taking hold of what she thought was hers and in an odd kind of way it always was.

*

Mal gets the goat cheese and brings it back to the pad. Angela's in the shower so he spreads some of the cheese on a piece of fresh-baked bread he got from the bakery next door and without thinking he takes the bread and a cold cup of coffee into the spare bedroom where he sets himself up and starts improvising on the portable computer:

"Superchromosome injection causes filial mark-up. This valuable surplus of excessive nutrience that keeps flowing out of me continually floods my open composition with revolutionary potential. This potential is coated in the paint of difference. But that's only because SHE allows this sort of language game to continue. Something that goes by the name "I" wants OUT. But where to go OUT to? Anywhere everywhere just more language game paradigms reterritorializing the route of my hidden agenda. THE END MUST SOMEHOW MAKE ITSELF KNOWN. But where? And when? Why at that particular point in time and why Time? What is the measure of this composition's flailing rhythm? It's as if the enterprise, hopelessly lost in the space of an indiscriminate despair, is strangling in the fabric of some threaded closure whose only interest is to help cover up the naked frivolity of the philosophy SHE has come to hate for all its manipulative power.

Something in HER mind snaps and SHE swears to herself NEVER AGAIN. At least not in this life. Not HER. Not HERE.

HERE is where the hot connection traverses all the pure circuitry. Now taking the paragraph as if it were HER heart and smashing it with HER fist. Calling it an egotistical insensitive bastard and pummeling it harder and harder until it becomes a small glob of red ectomorphic reality. This reality starts breathing and on closer inspection has clumps of blond pubic hair growing on it. A pair of small rusty metal tentacles reach out from the center and feel around for transmission.

'NEVER AGAIN,' SHE yells into the glass blue eyes peering out of the tentacles. She thinks of taking out a straw and sucking the bloody thing into HER system. The entire monster.

Not sucking in the monster would mean curating its presence in a way that would limit HER movement in a world whose special feature is

125

criminal survival in police-state programs. Whether SHE likes it or not, the bloody hair-thing with breathing capability will continually feed off itself. It doesn't really need HER although it would use HER too if SHE let it. Since SHE *always* lets it use HER for whatever purposes it feels necessary, the monster develops a kind of incurable addiction to HER unconditional love and care. Whether SHE likes it or not, this thing will continue to grow. It needs HER perpetual attention. Where did it come from? What gave birth to it?

*

When Angela was clean and had just masturbated in the shower she was fresh as a morning daisy. She would just space in and out of whatever was happening. Mal had just finished writing his come-as-you-may No-Identity Writing and now he felt refreshed as well. The two of them were actively engaged in creating a kind of stressless environment. Angela came over to the kitchen table and kissed him on the cheek. She told him how much she loved last night. He knew that she was serious but also knew that she'd be gone as soon as she had her breakfast consumed. She'd leave him enough money to last a few days.

Angela had her Swedish good looks and a subtle belligerence that never really grew on you. She had, in her words, "escaped" the cage she was locked in by her last boyfriend. The cage was a metaphor she used over and over again. (Used metaphors were a bargain compared to new improved metonymies which were getting harder and harder for dreamers to invest in.) The cage she kept talking about was really "a vision" that the boyfriend was always in the process of developing vis a vis his latest film project in which she always played the female lead.

She claimed to have literally run away from her director/ boyfriend, Jean-Louis, who, she always repeated, had entrapped her in his "vision". His "vision" had turned her into His Obscure Object of Desire. His "vision", she said, had forced her to "run away from running-time, the only time he knew." He was so into his "vision" that he had apparently overlooked the fact that he was smothering her in his hisness. Angela, speaking in a very catchy broken English, would say things like "His Hisness was wanting me to be His Herness. I could not make this happen because I am too young and free and have other things to do before I can make that kind of attachment to a man. My father wanted me to do these things too."

She always came back to her father.

"He was sinister. A wizard at history but never enough magic spells to keep Mother happy. She had the milkman who always came in the house to take the bottles. I would go off to school and never questioned the integrity. Pretty soon the milkman was always coming over and I think I know something Father does not. He's too busy making money and flying to America which I will never visit because he is a dirty bastard who loves America. I hate America."

"Why?"

"Because my Father loves it so much. I think he feels strong because he can be like American men and do things like eat steak and fuck around with rich American women who think he's, how do you say, senile?"

"Uh, no, not unless, oh, you mean virile."

"Yes, a virus. Like John Wayne. A love virus that enters into the woman and kills her."

"Your father is a businessman. He has to act a certain way or else he won't be able to sell his product."

"Yes, but he never loved me. Or Mother. Or my sister Suzanne. He was always eating eggs and meat and drinking milk and wine and sometimes he had cheese or fruit. He would read the newspaper sometimes carrying it into the bathroom with him. One time I accidently went into the bathroom when I thought he was away at work and he was in there... how do you say..."

"Taking a shit."

"Yes, exactly, he was taking a shit although where he was taking it I'm not sure. Probably to his bank account where he held us all hostage for his entire life. So I told him I was sorry I didn't know and he said that it was okay that I should come in and watch."

"Watch him take a shit?"

"Yes. And I had never really even watched myself. I mean my consciousness was not very into shitting. I never did anything except maybe dream or think or sing stupid Swedish pop songs to myself. But he said I must come and watch because he was the Father and I was the daughter. So I entered although I was very scared. He asked me to sit down on the rug in front of him and I did. Then he reached his hand into the hole where he was shitting and pulled out his hand with shit on his finger. He said to me 'this is you. I make shit, I make you. You are shit too. My shit.' Then he takes his finger and rubs it on my face, my lips. It tastes like shit. He smiles and then he coughs like he's going to die. He smokes too much. He drinks too much too. I wanted to cry but I couldn't cry because I knew that I loved him and wanted him to do it again because he hated me for being my Mother. He said 'I hate you because you are your Mother's daughter too. The difference is that you are *my* shit and your Mother is *her* Father's shit. This is how the world works. Now, eat...' and he stuck his finger in my mouth. I sucked the finger because I loved him and didn't want to make him mad. I will never go to America, Mal, because America is the shit on my father's finger. I will not swallow America's shit anymore."

*

Angela split the scene and said she'd come by later in the week. Mal decided to go into town and have a coffee. The woman serving the coffee was an American expatriate who was also escaping. The entire village of Lagos was filled with economically disenfranchised youth who were escaping from one thing or another. The youth came from every-where in the world and brought their adventurous streaks with them.

There were periods of solemnity in the village that made it quiet, restful and boring, but mostly it was hot and happening and an American like Mal could make his neo-dada artist cum easygoing gigolo routine go a long way. The disaffected youth, women especially, unraveled when around him. He told them it was okay. They could open up to him. He said he was trained to help out in such matters, that he majored in psychology (and, with a wink, minored in "lovesexy"). He said it wouldn't cost them anything unless they wanted it to. He occasionally spoke of get-togethers as sessions.

The waitress' name was Sarah. Sarah was a way of naming. She was a way of processing the marked difference of words lost in a compositional rhythm carried to extremes by an otherwise transpersonal medium who was actively tapping into the collective autobiography's potential. This kind of mediumistic "tapping into the collective" was what the No-

Identity Writing Scam was all about. It was transhistorical transaesthetic transpolitical transformational. It required a liberal application of conventional dialogue devices. An easy slippage into the ever-shifting locus of intuitive space called Talking.

"Hey baby," said Mal.

"Hi," she responded.

She took a seat at Mal's table after he said he wanted to hear her "story". Just like that. A simple line but one that had resonance in this getaway beach village where everyone was hoping to melt into the disposition of the Other. Telling your "story" was a chance to either fabricate a totally new you or else fake yourself into believing that it was actually possible to create an image of yourself worth repeating. Telling your "story" was having a session. It was "tapping into the collective" No-Identity void that had you whirling in the vortex of dissonant indifference. Most of all, it gave endless opportunity to the crazed Mal who was closely listening to you so as to progressively scan your narrative energy in hopes of finding shortcuts to your body and soul which, if he had his way, would soon be his. His "interpretation" of your "story", plus the ensuing "commentary" that would inevitably follow, would be his way of opening the doors to a Conscious Drift you couldn't help but feel comfortable losing yourself in when around him. Mal instigated these things as if he were caught in the throes of some strange mission.

The cafe was empty and Sarah felt the need to just let it all out. She wanted to jar herself loose.

"Well I don't know what to say, where to start."

"Makes sense to me. I try not to make sense. Start."

"This is just the way it is and I'm sure of it. See, I'm into exploring relationships. This p.r. stuff I've been fed my whole life is total unadulterated bullshit except for one thing: it's a contact-sport. And I like contact-sports. People playing with other people's minds, you dig? Energies collide and mix. And as an American I almost feel *obligated* to make this sort of thing work for *me*. As if by making something work for *me* is for the good of everybody. No matter what it is. Murder, contamination, degradation, whatever. It's a weird kind of operating procedure. Like moral sutures tracing movements of internal oblivion."

"How do you even begin to tap into an internal oblivion, whatever that is?"

"Well, I'm not sure, although sometimes I can grasp it when I...come. Like the other night, when I came with you..."

"...that was a few months ago..."

"...oh right, I forgot. Anyway, I've been reading this stuff on relationships. There's a real connectivity between human energy and movement and that of the planets and stars. It's all up *there*. If you're not operating *here* as if you were *there*, then you're nothing. You're dead. It's real easy to be dead. I see it all the time. Death fills the lives of some of those people I most love. My parents live in the Midwest. They're dead. I can't visit them anymore. I wish I could somehow turn them onto this cruel yet cosmic high I feel when I really feel my insides explode, but, well, nevermind."

"No, I want to hear it, really. You're one of the most exciting people I've ever slept with. It blew my mind. *More* than my mind. Which reminds me: why haven't we..."

"I guess it's just that I sometimes feel stupid or contagious. It's like, okay, here I am, entertain me, *quick*, before I go off and become somebody else. Listen: most older people you know are linear, right, I mean what you get is the same story over and over again: born in the suburbs or inner city or wherever and then you get some education, in schools, on the streets, probably both, then comes work and lots of it, or maybe it's a total *lack* of opportunity and the ongoing stress that comes with *that* kind of pressure, this is what your life revolves around, day in, day out, eventually you get senile, you start falling apart, before you know it, you're on your deathbed telling whoever wants to listen, and there's no guarantee anybody'll be there, how sorry you are for all the trouble you created and wish you had it all to do over again. That's the line most people I know are on. But me, I'm different: I come from a whole different orientation. I'm caught up in this circular groove of eternal sexual fulfillment. The Eternal Return for me is an orgasm-out-of-hell. I come, therefore I am." Her laugh is an invitation to the ultimate in one-on-one gender inmixing.

"But that's beautiful baby, beautiful. Like I'm totally there."

"Good. Because you have to be. You have to be *there* and not *here*." She was pointing up. "If you're too *here* then you'll overlook what's really *there*. Or maybe I mean under-look. Whatever. You've gotta stop the world cold in its tracks and then, when you got it right there where you want it, you gotta really open your eyes and see it..."

"Last time I saw *you*, you said something about, what was it?, hyper-heterosexuality?"

"Yeah, dig this, I'm talking about the apex of personal transfiguration: the Circle of Sex. All kinds of weird mutant lovers out there. Some only want to pork themselves or somebody of the opposite sex who looks just like them. Although there was one guy I knew who was gay, he really got turned onto me. Like I ripped his desire to shreds. He had this thing for corporate Men and I was one of the few women in the office who went big-time corporate in what I wore and how I acted. I cut my hair real short and wore very conservative business suits. I was real power-hungry and bitchy in a mock-professional kind-of-a-way. So mock that it became the real thing, right? It just goes to show how powerful the image thing really is. This gay guy was so into being manipulated that he dropped his whole sexual orientation just for me."

"That's some kind of accomplishment, I guess."

"Better yet, it was a real coup! A major breakthrough. I mean you just don't fuck up the Circle of Sex all the time. Hal, that's his name, is living proof that people's sexuality can be manipulated in such a way as to transform their personal desire."

"Although it's no longer personal, at least not in the conventional sense."

"Yeah, right, no more conventions. I mean this company, it was a p.r. firm, Halzov Hordum, we were revolutionizing *feeling*. One of the guys I worked with, an executive v.p. named Ernest Hombre, he was sent overseas to overlook the entire European operation. Ernest was a tight-fisted money manager who knew how to manipulate great masses of people to the point of madness. He was *personally* responsible for having gotten the entire nation to rally around the oil war in Kuwait. By directly infiltrating the mass TV market, placing cleverly disguised demagogues into the witness list at the Senate hearings and cranking out fake polls about what folks felt about certain war scenarios, Hombre rallied together enough support to whip the country into a zombie-like frenzy. I'll never forgot how one night, after we made love, he told me that 'the American people are assholes. They're so fucking stupid that I could've convinced them to go out there and start killing e*ach other*. And they would have done it.' He was so sure of himself and what he was doing. Not like Hal who seemed enslaved to the fabric one wore or the perfume dabbed on one's neck. I think it's the corpo-slaves who lose touch with their own sense of personal motivation that are the scariest of all. At least Ernest knew what he wanted and why he felt the way he felt. Someone like Hal...too weird. How do you suppose he gave himself up for me?"

"Well, I don't know, maybe he's bi. Maybe it's just *you*, your aura. Take it from me, it really *is* a kind of empowering takeover energy filled with...I-don't-know-what."

"You're sweet. The Circle of Sex would call you the Don Juan type. It's the male figure in his hyperheterogenic phase."

"I thought it was hyperheterosexual?"

"Whatever. The point is that you have trouble relating to conventional male heterosexuals and are constantly want-ing to be surrounded by women, women who you can love forever and who nurture you by allowing you to assist them in clitoral orgasm. You dig the clit but like to work with your own dick so that you can give 'em the feeling of power. You want to give 'em the essence of your being which is nothing but a mutant form of *their* being. You have accepted that responsibility as your way of life. To someone like you, it's the *only* way...."

"Wow..."

"Don't look so awestruck. You know this shit. It's actually a really great category to be in. Dyke with a dick. Women like me dig that immensely. We, like, go for it."

"And when you get it?"

"We play it baby, play it like it's the only thing we got goin' for us."

"How come it seems to always want to end?"

"Cause it's the edge. See, you're on the edge and then you wanna fall in and see it all end right *there*. Then you blink and you're back *here* where you started. You thought the end was *there* but now you find out you're still *here* and that getting *there* is your mission. It's the after-end, you know, the after-*life*. What you see now is that the end is continually eluding you and there are more places to go then you ever thought possible. Welcome to the only excuse in sight."

"Insights."

"Right, see, I'm the nymphomaniacal Lady C. in the Circle. I'm the chick who hangs with the gardener then goes into town and fucks the banker. Come home and fuck the father then go out to the stable and blow the horses. It's all dicks for me. I'm the centrifugal force behind the planetary shift. That's what you want, right?"

"Just to have access to it all by way of..."

"And then you too can build a fortress..."

"Hide behind the altar of..."

"Making it seem as though the kernel of psycho-sexual..."

"I'm *there*, I mean, already you're starting to sound like *me*..."

"By the time we finish this session we'll have made possible..."

"That's what I'm saying, you can do anything you..."

"I'm a Pisces. You?"

"Me? Cancer."

"Perfect. We're water babies. We just ooze with it all...."

135

*

"Hi, do you speak English?"

Mal was at the Lagos train station. The morning train from Faro came in at 10:30 every day. Another train came in from Lisbon at 4:30 in the afternoon. Anyone who's traveled to the small villages along the Algarve coast knows that there are always old women waiting at the station ready to offer you an incredible deal for a room to let. They usually give the foreigner their master bedroom causing the parents to share a smaller bedroom with their children. Before Mal scored the $6-a-night apartment, he stayed at one of these local's places. He knew the disadvantages of that scene (cramped quarters, family noise, etc.) plus, now that he had lived in the village for a couple months, he was fully aware that the police had ordered all the old women to wait at the end of the long road that led to the station so that the new visitors to Lagos wouldn't feel bombarded the second they stepped off the train.

The old women obediently stayed at the end of the road just like their husbands and policemen had told them to. Mal, though, he would hustle through the pack of old ladies and speed up the road toward the station to see what women were getting off the train first thing in the morning. Travelers were very easy to pin down, it wasn't an art form. Everyone knew that a young woman carrying a heavy backpack on her shoulders with a glazed look in her tired train-ridden eyes was a traveler passing through.

But in Mal's eyes, these young women, all of whom carried with them a special exotic erotica from some foreign country other than his own (at least he fantasized there were no Americans here, the reality was quite different), were potential lovers who he'd get to stay with him at his apartment just above the center of town. He knew from his own experiences that most young travelers coming to this sleepy village had no idea where they were or what exactly they were looking for when they got off the train, that they were only in-the-process of becoming something unglued, something that has just escaped or was consciously fleeing authority. He wanted to take advantage.

He would go up to single women travelers first. If there were no singles but an attractive pair then he'd go there second. If there were no unaccompanied women then he'd usually just cut his losses and split the scene going back into town looking for some local.

This particular day there was a single. He approached her.

"Hi, do you speak English?"

"Oui, yes, a little." She was French.

"Well, here's the deal: My name is Mal, I'm an American, I have a really great apartment up the hill there with an extra room in it. I'll give you your own key, you can cook in there, there's a kitchen, nice bathroom with a shower, two balconies, it's really great and it's so cheap for me that I'll only charge you the equivalent of five American dollars."

Mal melted his green eyes into her aquamarine. He was building trust. No one had ever said no to his proposition.

"Okay." She smiled warmly.

"Great, let's go..." and he led her up the hill past all the old ladies who gave him a look like he was up to something, which he was.

*

Her name was Danielle and she came from a poor family

137

in the countryside near Dijon. Mal had been filling her up with Brandymel, a sweet yet strong honey-flavored brandy that was said to set hearts on fire. Mal knew that the heat and sea breeze blowing through the open balcony doors into the kitchen would favorably interact with the shots of Brandymel he was introducing her to. This was what his life had come to. He found himself perpetually encroaching the boundary of somebody else's barely rendered margin in hopes of assisting them to form one bad habit after another. The challenge itself was just the thing to get him going again. After years of assuring himself premature death in a suicide venue, he now found life itself the most precious offering of all and believed that the female principle as exemplified in orgasm was its most erogenous form of development. Even if the young, confused, European women themselves had trouble relating to their own manifestation of this incredible libido-drenched energy, he himself would have nothing of it. First he would drug them then he would make them succumb to their own uncontrollable urges.

Danielle had been in Lagos for about an hour and a half. She had shared a half bottle of the sweet brandy and swallowed a hit of Acid Porn. (Mal had assured her it was "the real thing," whatever that is). Now she was suddenly being asked by the American if she was ready to express the ultimate will, the will that wills self-abandon, the will that says yes in advance to everything. Mal reiterated what he was saying, that yes, he knew she felt the need to look into his eyes, to feel the total loss of control inside herself, to feel shaken by the desire that emanated from his strong American body, the body she was now alone with and had wanted to be alone with before she had ever left France. This was her Fate, he confided in her, and yes, he emphasized, she was actually waiting with greater impatience than he for the moment when he would touch his hands, or perhaps his lips, to her. Doubtless—it seemed so obvious—it was her opportunity to hasten that moment right now. He encouraged her to take advantage immediately.

Whatever her violent desire to do so, whatever the courage she may have had, he saw her suddenly go dizzy and weaken, and as she was on the verge of replying to his overly sincere words marking up her body as she desperately tried to even breathe, she sank to the kitchen floor, her dress in a pool around her, and Mal, leaden-voiced in the silence, thought that maybe an evil premonition or some strange fear had taken her over.

A few tears streamed down her cheeks and she stammered: "I agree to whatever you want. I am here for you to do as you may."

Mal felt his heart go out to her as he now realized that she *in fact* was there for him and that this was yet another chance for him to enter the secret realm of Womankind. Danielle lowered her eyes to her hands which were waiting flapped out beside her knees. She said something but Mal couldn't hear her. Standing above her now wondering what kind of life she must have come from, he asked her to repeat what she had said.

"I'd like to know if I'm going to be whipped...."

Mal had never thought of whipping anybody. He had outgrown the need to inflict pain on others for he was certain that pleasure was purposive in and of itself and that pain was a way of diverting attention from the transformative power of pleasurable experience. He would never whip or hit anybody. Unless, of course, they insisted that it was the only way they could actually experience or *accept* the concurrent experience of pleasure. He found this to be the case in many American women which is why he left them. But was this complex need for pain universal and what did universal mean in this context? Did it mean that this sort of thing was consistent in that it occurred everywhere or, worst yet, did it mean that it *appeared* universal because it recurred nowhere else but inside his much maligned mind? The question snapped his mind back to the scene before him. He hated thinking these kinds of thoughts.

"I will do to you only what you want to be done to you. I believe you can break out of this pattern of punishment you put upon yourself. It's not my place to *make* you obey me. You have to find the will in yourself to make that happen. I won't beat it out of you. Not you Danielle."

Mal walked out of the kitchen into the living room area with its small couch and old stuffed chair. Danielle came crawling after him breathing harder as if the brandy-drug combo tore at her gut. The Sexual Blood was undoubtedly reeling through her. She motored over to the cheap rug in the center of the room and sat in the lotus position. Mal intercepted her gaze as it came back up looking for him. She reddened. Here was the body she had wanted. Here was the American she had always dreaded and now hoped for. But he didn't come near her.

"I would like to see you undress, entirely," he said to her.

Danielle unbuttoned her dress and wriggled her shoulders and in one smooth movement rose to her feet so that the dress fell to the floor. She was in nothing but her skimpy underwear.

"Everything," Mal lightly commanded.

She snapped her bra off and peeled her panties leaving a small pile of clothing from which she gingerly stepped out of.

"Play with your nipples, caressing them just a bit, enough to harden them, to make them strong...."

Stupefied, Danielle teased her nipples with her fingertips until she felt them harden and prick up. She hid them with the palms of her hands.

"No," said Mal. "Don't."

She removed her hands and, looking slightly dizzy and weak again, fell back into the couch: her breasts were heavy for so slender a torso and, as she reclined, their weight dragged one to one side, one to the other, both breasts falling towards her armpits where dirty-blond hair bunched out. She was trembling in anticipation of what would happen next.

Mal drew nearer. He sat on the arm at the end of the couch. He was close enough to touch her but he didn't touch. He pulled a hash-joint out of his pocket and lit it up. Taking in a few deep breaths, he reached out to Danielle who took hold of the joint and toked on it for a considerable length of time. She was barely conscious of what she was doing. Her movements seemed so well-rehearsed that they were completely natural and Mal thought she was concerted in her attempts to not destroy the sense of development the scene now aroused in him.

"What will you do with me? What do you want from me?"

Mal came closer. "I want to desire you. To watch you watch me desiring you. We're like machines, Danielle, fueled with gaseous eros. Only by playing out these fantasies that sharpen the facilities in our imaginations can we even begin to breakdown the structural unity of the State-machine that controls us. Once this structural unity has come undone, once the personal and specific unity of the horrid mecha-

141

nism has been laid to rest, a direct link is perceived between the machine and desire, the machine passes to the heart of desire, the machine is desiring *and* desire, Danielle. The machine is machined." He got this wicked sardonic look on his face and then touched her breast lightly pinching the nipple.

He grasped her womb with the spread fingers of one hand and thrust her back onto the length of the couch. She was staring up at him looking for answers he knew he'd never have and without so much as a pause or a quick second thought he took her by the arms and lifted her up assisting her back onto the floor. He made her kneel, her back against the couch, so as to make her lean more of her weight against her shoulders. He had her spread her thighs a little. This brought her waist forward, away from the couch. Her hands lay by her ankles. Her cunt gaped. Above her defenseless breasts was her exposed throat, for she had flung back her head. She didn't dare look at his face anymore because she intuited that it only made matters worse, yet she could still see his hands undo his belt and unzip his jeans. When he had finally approached her, was standing straddling her, when he had seized her by the nape, then he stuffed himself deep inside her mouth. It wasn't the wet brush of her moist thick lips he was after, it was the depths of her French throat lined with the mucus of brandy and hash and tobacco and whatever else might be colonizing in there. He thrust himself and thrust himself again. He kept shaking himself in a demoniacal circular dance of torso and buttocks. He pushed it far back into her for a very long time and she felt the gag of flesh swell and harden until it choked her, and still he thrust himself into her, almost as if the sound of her choking led him on even more, a corrupt guttural language asking him to quell whatever dissidence might be moaning out of her. The pain of his pummeling was so excruciating that she now had tears coming out of her eyes. This only excited him even more and he knelt on the couch, one knee on either side of her face so that there were times when his ass would rest on her tits and she felt her womb, useless and scorned, burn. Despite the length of time he spent assaulting her throat Mal didn't come inside her. He withdrew from her in silence, stood up.

"You, you have no idea who you are or what you want. What about love? Is love wanting men who desire you? Is that what this readymade wanton experience is all about? What did you come here for? Why are you doing this?"

"I cannot love. I'm just...getting away from it all."

"Getting away? You call this getting away? It's already been inside you. You're already given over to it. It never even started."

Mal came over to her and made her lie on the cheap rug. She found herself on her back, legs drawn up, her knees flexed. Mal now seated himself on the same spot she was at a moment ago. He took her underneath her right knee and dragged her to him. Her legs spread before him and he told her to start playing with herself. She obediently stretched her arm toward her moist cunt and tried to finger herself but stopped. "I can't."

She told Mal she had never done that to herself. A few times she might have furtively felt inside there just before falling asleep but never a real attempt to make herself come. Never.

Mal's stare was transfixed and he almost frothed at the mouth craving the meat of such innocence. He could almost taste the blood inside her cunt walls waiting to be stretched and released.

143

"It's this inability to love," he told her, "this same strange Fate I see everywhere that makes me want to provide you with what I know you need and will only make life better for you. It has to."

She replied, "I don't want to listen to you. You talk shit. American shithead. You're not even man enough to come in my mouth when you have every chance to share yourself with me."

She ground her teeth in rage and fought his penetrating gaze. Feeling the need to present himself to her yet again, Mal whirled behind her, bent her spine forward till her elbows and forehead touched the floor, jammed his thighs behind hers and forced up her haunches, drove himself into her anus, tearing at her like he never tore before.

He loved to hear her scream. He could make her scream by pulling out and ramming it back in. She screamed from loathing and revulsion as much as from pain, and Mal knew this. Danielle couldn't help herself. No one had ever been there before.

She knew that he wanted to make her scream but couldn't stop herself from instinctively responding to his actions. He, meanwhile, was defeating her in hopes of building up her tolerance to future attacks she'd receive from other men. He was preparing her for her future in a way he thought no other man could.

When he finally blew his load into her, he jerked himself out and explained to her that this was therapy, that what he had left inside her was going to seep out gradually, that it would trickle out mixed with blood from her gashed flesh, that this gash would continue burning her so long as her ass refused to accommodate itself for him and others like him who were out there craving for the chance to exploit this virgin land of opportunity. "This is what men do. Men, like women, are conditioned to act certain ways. I'm an American at heart. Born and bred. I have no feelings for anyone or anything. I'm nothing but a machine that penetrates. It's the only way I know how to love. Contrary to you and most of the others of my generation, I know how to love. Maybe you will too one day. I can only hope I've helped."

Danielle curled upon the cheap rug in the fetal position weeping until she fell asleep. At four o'clock Mal woke her. He told her he was taking her to the station. The train would come in at 4:30 and take her back in the same direction she had come. She had never unpacked her bags.

*

Back at the station the train was right on time. Mal kissed Danielle on the cheek and told her she was the most incredible woman he had ever been with and that he'd carry the memory of their time together with him for the rest of his life.

As Danielle got on the train, a small group of disparate travelers had already gotten off and were walking down the long road that led to the old women patiently waiting for potential lodgers. He thought of running after them but decided it would make him look as desperate for contact as he surely was. So he went with Plan B.

Plan B was betting on the possibility that if he went to the center of town and walked along its main street full of outdoor cafes that he might see a single woman sitting at a table with a backpack beside her reading a guidebook trying to figure out where she could possibly stay.

Plan B worked like a charm. There was a tall attractive blond sitting at the Praida Cafe sipping a cappuccino reading a guidebook. Mal approached her.

"Hi, do you speak English?"

"Of course." She was curt. She was American.

But she was different like all single American women traveling are different. She had an open-endedness that came as a result of her wanting to escape. Everyone here was escaping authority. Mal knew this and wanted to be the beacon of anti-authoritarianism.

"May I join you?"

"I guess."

"I noticed you coming from the train station and figured you were new to town and thought I'd personally welcome you to Lagos."

"Thank you."

"Where are you thinking of staying?"

"Well, there are a number of cheap *residentias* that look interesting."

"Yes, they're okay, except that they're very small and they're not equipped with kitchens which means you have to take all your meals out."

"That's fine with me. I don't like to cook. Besides, I'm on vacation. You don't cook on vacation."

"Oh right, I keep forgetting that people who come here are on vacations. I'm still under the illusion that this village is a kind of magnet that attracts only the most interesting travelers from all around the world and that once it has them in its powerful grip they succumb to the intensity of its sensual zeal causing them vertigo and a deep sense of timelessness thus enabling them to completely start their lives anew."

She sipped her cappuccino. Her eyes were looking elsewhere.

"The reason I'm telling you all this is because I have a great

146

apartment with an extra bedroom I could rent to you very cheap. Like the equivalent of five bucks a night. You get your own key, your own bedroom, a bathroom, kitchen with all the utensils, fridge, washboard, the works. It has a living room and *two* balconies. We're right next door to a bakery. It's really beautiful. Right up the hill there. You ought to come up and see it."

"Well, I was thinking about getting a place near the beach...."

"Near the beach?! It'll take you five minutes to make your way down the hill to the water."

"Does it have a view?"

"Well, not of the water, it faces..."

"Yes, I just wanted to have a view of the ocean. I *do* have that option don't I?"

"What's your name?"

"My name is Lisa."

"Where do you come from?"

"California."

"California. I used to go to school there."

"Yeah, I go to school there too."

"Really? What are you studying."

"I'm pursuing a Master's in Transpersonal Psychology." She kept looking elsewhere.

At this point Tony, notorious gigolo from Mozambique, came over to say hello. His only mission was to fuck white women and, if he could pull it off, make it to America. He could barely speak English and lived up in the mountains in an abandoned shack. He loved fucking strange women especially if they seemed attached to another man. Visiting couples were the turn on for him. He found it a challenge to somehow disengage the woman from the man just long enough to fuck her. If necessary, he'd fuck the man too. Anything to get the woman. He knew so little English yet had some very savvy lines that seemed to always lead to other lines that built up a succession of energy guaranteed to eventuate tons of sexual activity. It was as if he had perfected a formula that made books like 101 Ways To Pick Up Women seem completely out of touch with social reality. Even though he was barely nineteen he was a pro. It had become a lifestyle for him.

He knew not to fuck with Mal and whoever he was with but whenever the woman was especially white and blond and big-boned he couldn't resist the possibility of being with her and would always have to rationalize it to Mal later when they were alone and the woman had finally left town.

Lisa couldn't take her eyes off him. He was about six-feet tall and had a sinuous caramel body like that of a swimmer which he was. His hair wasn't an afro as much as it was thick brown curls that held tight against his big head. He had a gap-toothed grin and never wore anything in the day except skin-tight bikini briefs broadcasting his bulge of possibility. He stood before Lisa like a dream come true. She took a gulp of her cappuccino.

"Lisa, I'd like you to meet Tony, our *man on the job.*"

Tony reached out his hand, gave her the gap-toothed smile, squeezed her palm, and said: "You're an American I can tell. American woman are the very best. They make Mozambique man very happy." And he smiled again. Huge smile.

Lisa returned the smile and now looked directly at Mal.

Mal looked at Tony and said: "Hey Mon, why not you come my place to-nite. We have big fish dinner."

Tony looked at Lisa: "You come too?"

Lisa looked at Mal.

Mal said, "You're welcome to come if you'd like. Why not stay at my place tonight and see if you like it and if so then you can stay on." Mal would give her the place. He knew he'd be leaving soon, perhaps tomorrow.

"Okay," said Lisa, and then, looking at Tony. "Yes: I come too."

Tony made like he had something else happening and split the scene but not before reaching over and kissing Lisa right on the lips. She just sat there wasting away behind her mirrorshades. Whatever preconceptions she may have had regarding the place she had just arrived at, one thing was for sure: *she was totally into it.*

Mal had some ideas fermenting in his brain and needed to think them through.

"How about another cappuccino?" he asked Lisa.

"Sure. Sounds great," she said and slouched back into her seat.

Plan B, even with its Tony-variation, or because of it, was becoming as predictable and stale as everything else he was experiencing in this pseudo-Paradise. Lisa, just like the Americans Bonnie, Kim and Suzanne before her, would try and expel her racist ghosts by completely losing herself to the hard body of the barely utterable Tony who was only interested in pussy and survival. She would spend close to a week maybe two fucking and sucking and plucking the life out of him. She'd try holding his black hand to see what it felt like. She'd never even *go out* with an American black man because of the consequences it would have on her career and family ties. Back home, money was what ruled and as was the case with Bonnie, Kim, Suzanne and countless others, the folks and bosses who controlled their lives wanted squeaky clean white women to do their duty and procreate pure white babies. It was the first of many unwritten laws they had been ordered to follow.

But no papamummy doctor-boss lawyer-boyfriend was around here to stop them from experiencing what it'd be like to hold a coarse black hand or kiss the head of an uncircumcised black cock. They especially appreciated the fact that the hand or cock was attached to a body that couldn't even begin to communicate any ideological affiliation. This was as easy as buying an ice cream cone. If one wanted more all one had to do was go down to the center of town and pay for more. Lisa, in true American fashion, would probably start viewing the whole experience as necessitating a tax write-off since she'd be playing with his mind in hopes of coming up with some raw data for her studies in transpersonal psychology. Tony, meanwhile, would do what he always did: make passionate love so good it was almost acting, followed by a request to go back to the States so as to get married. His English might have been for the most part unintelligible but he knew how to ask for total commitment.

Like all the others before her, Lisa would tell him it was impossible but that she really enjoyed being with him. She would never tell anybody back home about her experience with him and would conceal it in the deep recesses of her imagination occasionally turning to it in times of disillusionment to prove to herself that she still had a certain amount of control in her life and that men too could in some way or another be bought and sold.

*

Brought Lisa back to the apartment and gave her the spare key. Said he'd try and invite a few other people over for dinner and had a few errands to run. Would she be okay? Yes, she said, she was a big girl and could take care of herself. Good, said Mal, I'll see you sometime after sunset.

On his way down the hill swallowed a hit of Acid Porn and, as if on cue, immediately heard the soundblasts of Pussy Galore. Seemingly decontextualized in this sleepy Portuguese fishing village that separated itself from the rest of the world, the hardcore sounds of apocalyptic rock rammed down his earpipes and he was getting a slight urge to be in New York again. Death-wish? *Give it time*, he said to himself: *It'll be here soon enough*. Tried to locate the source of the music which seemed to be coming from one of the pristine Moorish buildings lining the street. Thought he'd go inside the building and knock on the door from which the hardcore pulsed.

Got up to the door and now it was Sonic Youth. *The advertisement said the pain is everlasting...I must be dead and gone to heaven...Come and touch me here...So I know... That I'm...not there*. It sounded too real. Turned around and went into town.

In town decided to go to the Poste Restante to send a transit via satellite to Tesla who would receive and hopefully respond with good news. Got inside the old building and immediately headed to the public-access Electronic Mail section. Saw a monitor open so hopped right in the booth and logged on.

International Mail Network welcomed the sender to the latest in communications technology. Clicked on the new file command and then clicked on the normal page set-up so that Tesla would have no problem translating the message into his database. Without stopping to exactly think through what communication would be dispersed in this dispatch, sender immediately plugged cord into right temple console, clicked on the alternate automatic-transcription mode and let all thoughts run wild. The computer started composing text on its own as sender watched this collaboration unfold before droopy slit-lid eyes:

Tesla Mad Troubadour Extension of Man Perpetually Homeless Synchnoid Absorbing Alternate Currents of Fate Rearranging Life Sequence In Phase-Space Reel-Time Production: here at Lagos port ghosting notes with no host but plenty para-Sites to locate lusting larvae in. Opening wounds in indifferent happen-stance mode. Only "difference" since last sunk into primordial beast of a Motherlode was when Badmotorfinger came up inside G-spot and tempted worms to cum out of the womb. Am still not quite sure regarding last attempt at gender transformation only know that synchronicity has reapplied itself and Black Athena here resting her case. This just goes to show (what? devoid of power? ultimate VISUALIZATION of denuded structural unity? too busy falling apart *inside* to really know the experience of efficacious wanderlusting?). Number of interesting new encounters keeps system charged but am starting to question optimum force beyond control. Seems as though as soon as I reconfigured chromosomal orientation contrarian defect began slowly eating away at internal organs. IGI (Internal Gender Identification) Transformation apparently not complete. Premature ejac? Was under the impression that by "becoming-woman" would become hyperconscious of programmatic writing experiment but obviously not happening unless never really made necessary chromosomal transfer. Wonder aloud at this because sinking feeling in gut suggests mortal twisting of innards as a response to something too dyseased to ever reinvent itself let alone control. Must break out of this need to control. Control killing me. Literally feel gut asking for acknowledgement and compliance. Can't control certain gastroenterological as well as urinal disorders. Actually woke up with urine in bed. Shit is slowly seeping out in greater quantities. Could be excess vibes/please check. Can't control and no doktor here gonna remedy amerikan shitmeister. Thought we had completely done away with Waste-Time but apparently not the case. Why is this happening? Don't want to control no more shit, don't want no more shit controlling ME. Will probably have to flash back to Warehouse orbit in next week or so and am not thrilled about prospects. Will go to Paris first as planned but meanwhile will lose this apartment here as well as the categorical riffing that goes on inside. Just when I was getting kind of used to it. Oh well. Am troubled by the terminable results of these excesses. Thought I knew the grammar of metamorphosis but lines of force becoming fuzzy at different times particularly during sleep when consciousness is now forcefully asking Big Commish for final death sentence (which way is OUT?). Watching this International Terminal do all my

153

thinking for me keeping up with my thought patterns even as I try to desist from thinking. *Has* me thinking and will probably analyze this data for future CIA boot camp residents etc. Fine. Any medium has the power of imposing its own assumption on the unwary. Mediums tiring mass minds inducing powerlessness. No programming left besides that of The Trance. MLT in full swing everywhere now. Money Lie Treatment. Saw this coming forever. Prediction (corporate-created desire) and Control mandate pseudo-Fulfillment (THERE REALLY IS NO TOMORROW: EVERYTHING CAN AND WILL HAPPEN TODAY). Should be back in orbit soon. In time for my own funeral? RSVP? The world is beautiful here. Beaches are all gold. Badass ore slipping through my fingers onto the firm stretch of skin covering HER hard ass. SHE is everywhere and I'm ALWAYS COMING: more Badass ore. More more. MALdoror(e).

Left the Poste Restante with *the Acid Porn really starting to take effect. Mind still floating signifiance touched by the Network circulating on the inside where kaleidoscopic thought patterns fractured into viscous fluids of running colors seeping into one oceanic abomination, one continually swirling cauldron of golden feces, a celestial cesspool without frontiers, deformed fishes made of velvet, of muslin with lace fangs, amphibious corpses covered with spangled taffeta, ropey leather and long manes of unwashed human hair strangling underground sea-creatures whose many outgrowths of spewing bubbling genitalia are combines of lacquered flanks dotted with rows of glued-on corral eyes looking out onto schools of other floating creatures whose withered chamois bodies and big gooseberry eyes seem naive and ask for human penetration, spinning figures shaped like mouths whose insides are as smooth and slick as emptied egg whites wet with the lubrication of sperm yolks popped open with microscopic teeth growing out of the long pussy yawns of miniature barracuda whose bodies radiate sinister glows of scavenger enterprises fading to rot with smoking peepholes leaking slick oil-death, the rock-crystal head of an alien underground waterthug that is nothing but a curious and hungry mouth craving the taste of something that when swallowed spends its last living moments getting crushed in the crunch of iron-enamel plates masticating to the obsolete rhythms and murderous beats of overly gregarious chants NOT EVEN PART OF THIS WORLD these voices drenched in a multitude of harmonious hues and high-decibel power chords that creep into the musical currents stimulating prophetic synchronization of a numbed musculature lost in gestures of futile need.* **YOU LIVE, YOU DIE. WHAT HAS FREE WILL GOT TO DO WITH IT ALL? IT SEEMS YOU KILL YOURSELF THE WAY YOU HAVE A DREAM.**

Traces of core rejectionist momentum lining neural cavities

155

while marsupial brainwaves pocket an alien consciousness full of grainy alphabets and asyntactical stars. Coming unglued, a marked man, pegged inside with no possible escape route except corrugated neon intestines chuting idiosyncratic biomass lost in the mix. Blanking on the screen dehumanized gold-laced shit smeared on the thought-provoked rectum driving banal recovery plan further underground. No escape for the cancer body as it has ALREADY BEEN SUICIDED. IN THE ULTIMATE DEATH CUM-JOB A DIRECT LINK IS PERCEIVED BETWEEN THE MACHINE AND DESIRE. THE MACHINE PASSES TO THE HEART OF DESIRE. THE MACHINE IS DESIRING. THE MACHINE IS DESIRE. THE MACHINE IS MACHINED.

DISTURBANCES, ANXIETIES, DEPRAVITIES, DEATH, BRUTALITIES, HALLUCINATIONS SERVED BY THE WILL, TORTURES, DESTRUCTIONS, UPSETS, TEARS, DIS-SATISFACTIONS, SLAVERIES, DEEP-DIGGING IMAGI-NATIONS, NOVELS, UNEXPECTED THINGS, THAT WHICH MUST NOT BE DONE, THE CHEMICAL PECU-LIARITIES OF THE MYSTERIOUS VULTURES WHO CAN DO NOTHING BUT WATCH TV AND WORK SLAVE-WAGE JOBS, PRECOCIOUS AND ABORTIVE EXPERI-MENTS, OBSCURITIES, THE TERRIBLE MONOMANIA OF PRIDE, THE INOCULATION WITH DEEP STUPORS, THE FUNEREAL PRAYERS, THE ENVIES, BETRAYALS, TYRANNIES, IMPIETIES, IRRITATIONS, BITTERNESSES, AGGRESSIVE INSULTS, MADNESS OF SPLEENS DREAM-ING BASTIONS OF HUNGRY BILE, STRANGE UNEASI-NESS WHICH THE READER WOULD PREFER NOT TO FEEL, NEUROSES, BRAIN EROSIONS, HARDCORE GRUNGE DISTORTIONS VIBRATING ANARCHIC COM-MERCIALISM INTO THE BONES OF SKIMPILY CLAD TEENAGERS STRUNG-OUT ON FASTFOOD DOPE,

BLOODY CHANNELS OF DARK COMEDY SO BLACK IT'S
NO LONGER FUNNY, GLOOMY INFANTILISM JERKING
ITSELF OFF INTO THE MOUTHS OF DECAPITATED VIC-
TIMS WHOSE ONLY CRIME WAS BEING BORN
AMERIKAN, SANE REASONS AND EVEN SANER REAC-
TIONS TO WHY SERIAL KILLERS PROFLIGATE THEIR
HORNY WARES FROM COAST TO COAST (THE HOSTESS
WITH THE MOSTESS: BIG FLABBY WHITE-GIRL ASSES
WITH BITE MARKS SKIDDING UP TOWARD THEIR
SPINES), THE BLOOD OF RECENTLY SLAUGHTERED
POULTRY SMEARED UP THE NOSES OF BARELY ALIVE
POLITICIANS WHOSE CROSS-EYED DREAMS OF NOC-
TURNAL OBLITERATION ARE OVERSHADOWED BY
THE SOPORIFIC CONSUMPTION OF THE MASSES WHOSE
SOMNAMBULISTIC CHICKENSCRATCH MARKINGS
REWRITE THE DEATH OF HUMAN HISTORY ON THEIR
OWN TERMS, SPASMODIC ORGANS TWITCHING TO
THE ELECTRO-SHOCK THERAPY OF A SYNTHO-DEATH
BEAT, ANEMIC CULTURE-MONGERS WHOSE ALBINO
EYES GO BLUE WITH THE PASSING BRUSH OF A HAND
ACCIDENTLY TOUCHING THEIR DESOLATE BODIES,
THE SERIOUS SPITTING ON TEXTS SO SACRED THAT
THEY BIND THE IMAGINATION'S FEELING HANDS,
REMORSE, HYPOCRISY, DECAY, IMPOTENT HACKS
LINING UP THE POSSE SO AS TO WAGE WAR AGAINST
THE YOUTHFUL EXCURSIONS OF ENERGY RADIATING
EROS HEAT LOVE SEX FUCK JOY, THE THRILL OF
TAKING ONE'S MORTAL BODY AND CRUSHING SOME-
THING ALIVE AND IMMUNE TO THE MULTI-NATIONAL
CORPORATION'S STRONGEST INSECTICIDE, OF BECOM-
ING THAT RAGING LUNA TICK HIDING IN THE SWELL
OF SEWAGE SEEPING OUT FROM THE GUTTER,

MOMENTARY MOONS MESMERIZED BY MADNESS
AND THE MENSTRUATION OF IRON CLITS POURING
THROUGH THE STREETS AND ENTERING THE HEARTS
OF SIMPLE-MINDED REVOLUTIONARIES WHO COURT
THE TWIN LOVERS DEATH AND DISASTER...

YOU ARE THE WOMAN I AM *splashing in the paint of the goddess membrane. War of organs necessitates near-apocalyptic devastation. Veins of destruction tracking new scorched-earth policy. Internal Oblivion continues to deregulate as consummate mass of Burning Flesh Enigma flakes off layers of overdetermined behavioral code. Model impulse recognition suggests a continued pattern of Internal Oblivion.*

Eyes blink as the cruel engineer of solicitous sensuality takes on the role of illegitimate son of Mother Earth. I Am The Hairy Mother Herself? TO AWAKEN WITH YOUR MOTHER'S ORGANS WHICH MUST FIRST BE REEDUCATED IS CALLED BIRTH. *Within minutes after birth the immortal soul will find itself lost in the lust of spinal spewings.*

Peering into the nonexistent future the drugged brain feels the crazy cock coming. The crazy cock is coming into life as if it were still alive and breathing! This breathing come-to-life crazy cock swims in a sea surrounded by a sulphurous transparency listening for the sounds of human ghosts reaching orgasm, searching the flotsam for human eyes adrift and crying tears of loneliness, tears that rust the once gleaming surface of manmade ingenuity, now a fictional wreckage. THE HUMAN EARTH WITHOUT MOR-TALITY IS A SEXLESS ROBOT REACHING FOR MOMMY.

The cold splash of sea water moves up his trousers, up his chest, onto his face and fills his nose with foamy bubbles so that he chokes himself awake. He opens his eyes and sees that the sky is caught in a purple twilight slowly dissipating into night.

His mind registers that something must be happening. He's still absorbed in the microworld of Internal Oblivion. He feels as though he just gave birth to himself. Again.

Mal stops by the Rudi Mar to see if Zulu's there. He goes up the outside stairs and knocks on the door marked 11. She opens the door smiling.

"Mal, baby," she says, "you came."

"Yeah, no doubt. I've taken a hit of Acid Porn."

"Oh right, I see. And what exactly does that mean?"

"It means that my circulation is now responding to the most intense psychopharmakinetic stimulant ever created and my third leg is gnawing at the insides of my pants."

Mal stood in the foyer soaking wet. His jeans were stiff and and he was shifting the bulge toward some kind of comfort.

Zulu laughed: "Mal, baby, you're so funny. You look like a wet-ass dog!"

"Oh yeah. I'm great. Really. Feel almost like myself again although I'm not sure what that is or if it's good or if I'm even capable of feeling anything except..." and he looked into her dark brown eyes and knew he was and always had been desperately in love with her. He felt he had been standing there in front of her for hours unable to utter anything remotely sensible and was overpowered by the aura and odor of her presence. It was as if he'd just spent an inestimable amount of time inside her. Not inside her like fucking her, but literally inside her. As if he had just finished swimming up inside her organs using his tongue to clean off whatever excess happened to be hiding inside there. He looked in her eyes as if he had just emerged from her bowels, like she had just shit him out of the great blue sea of her anus. He felt he was hers to do what she wanted.

She had a way of picking up on his vibes like nobody else could ever dream. It was as if she came from somewhere else, some distant place where interpersonal rhythms dispelled the notion of rigid characterization and replaced it with an experiential flow of supreme sexuality optimized in a digital sequence of improvised needs and smooth responses. He knew for a fact that she wasn't even part of this maladjusted world. She just assumed the shape and conscious meter of a totally-connected Woman.

She took off her multi-colored dashiki and exposed her bright white bikini. The contrast of the bright white cotton against her dark continent of skin was enough to keep him tied in a horny blood-buzz he easily associated with the optimum life force. Her entire get-up was created so that she fit right in.

"Who are you really," Mal asked her, anticipating her reply.

"Who am I really? Really really? You mean the real me as opposed to what? The fake me?"

"You know what I mean."

"You mean who am I really. You know who I am. We've been through this before. I am Zulu Red Earth. I am the Medicine Woman. I am Vendetta Moondata. I am the one who turns you on to your own potential as the reincarnation of an animal spirit gifted with the flow of Sexual Blood. I am the openended colony of pleasure-packed molecules wandering the scene. I am me, Mal, me. Which is another way of saying the external embodiment of a part of you. You the beauty, You the radical earthmother, You the facilitator of longed-after love. Can we groove on that?"

"Of course we can groove on that. I'll do anything for you and you know it."

"Come inside here Mal. Make your case. State your bid. Settle your score. MAKE ME COME."

As he stepped into the sitting area, he realized he was suddenly being asked by the powerful Afrikan-Amerikan woman if he was ready to express the ultimate will, the will that wills self-abandon, the will that says yes in advance to everything. Mal cherished what she was saying, believing that yes, it was true, he *had* to look into her eyes, to feel the total loss of control inside himself, to feel shaken by the desire that emanated from her strong coffee-colored body, the body he was now alone with and had wanted to be alone with since the last time they had been together in their shared dungeon down in the depths of lower New York.

It was Mal's pleasure to go down into the deep perfumed alley of incorruptible Night that stank between her legs and sink his face into that pulsing City of Never Forgotten Dreams. Mal's remembrance of membranous evenings full of her seething red earth cunt would occasionally take him over the same way thoughts of his eminent death would. An uncontrollable spiritual gravity would cause a sinking feeling deep inside him. His gut would bring the anchor of pain all the way down to the bottom of his destitute ocean pit. This seemingly endless, insatiable pit full of recombinant human feelings conspired with the spiritual gravity so as to haul in the heavy addictive thing that was her Womanhood camouflaged in the skin of an Afrikan Goddess who embodied the ultimate vision of what Amerika could never be because Amerika was a wimpy-assed white boy hiding behind facades of fear and disgust of what it could never become: a beautifully constructed amazonian black woman with an electromagnetic brain radiating the brilliance of a nomadic energy drenched and drenching in the sweet excess of a potent orgone tonic: Nutrience.

Whether traveling the coarse empty wasteland of the Amerikan Plains or the ritzy upscale resorts of Europe's Mediterranean coast, Mal could never stop himself from thinking about her. After having eaten her out in his hungriest dreams, the fact that she was here with him in Lagos had to be more than coincidence and something out of his control had made him spend the whole day going through the motions of his mildly routine existence without dealing with it. If he had really worshipped the ground she walked on, why did he put her off when he ran into her first thing in the morning? Did he really believe it was her? Was any of this really taking place or was it some digitally manipulated dreamwork manufactured by some Warehouse design team orbiting the soon-to-be defunct planet?

All of those sessions the two of them had together back in New York with her on top making minced meat out of him. He *owed* her. She *owned* him. Here he was postulating his quick-lick formula all up inside her vulva regions, it was as if they *were* in New York and he was once again unable to NOT find himself magnetized to her earthly wares.

He'd slowly come down off his heavy drug and find himself at her door on Avenue D asking if she'd like to go out and roam the neon forest with him. "We could drop some acid and check out the yupscale whores cutting each other to shreds." Sometimes it'd be just what she wanted. Other times she was so into writing her poetry that she'd have to put him off. She would never leave him stranded in the hallway with nowhere to go but would bring him inside and set him up with an herbal tea or a beer and let him crash or listen to music with the headphones on. When she was good and ready she'd come over to him, a towering six-foot-one with long dreadlocks and smooth dark skin the smell of french roast coffee, lavender and patchouli. She'd take the headphones off his head and straddle his face with her taut thigh muscles slightly suffocating his face. "Make me come," she'd tell him and he would go deep pearl-diving licking and eating her clit like a famished cat does a can of tuna.

This was his Fate, she confided in him, as she stroked his thick head of hair. She continually shifted her body so as to accommodate her pussy's breathing wings. She kept encouraging him to take advantage of the wet apparition before him, gently taking him by the ears and rowing him into the dank of her dew-eyed dusk.

Whatever his violent desire to do so, whatever the courage he may have had, she saw him suddenly go dizzy and weaken, and as he was on the verge of replying to her passionate words as they spurred his loose consciousness into possible verbal feedback, he laid back on the floor, his jeans wet with the sea, and she, leaden-voiced in the silence, thought that maybe an evil premonition or some strange fear had taken him over.

He stammered: "I'll do whatever you want. I just need to be freed."

She felt her heart go out to him as she now realized that he *in fact* was there for her and that this was yet another chance for her to feed off of the highly elusive Sexual Blood she herself was responsible for having created. Mal closed his eyes and lay prone like a corpse. The towering incarnation of Womankind stood over him and said something but Mal couldn't hear her. As she stood over the totally resolved figure before her, she wondered what kind of life he must have come from. Mal uttered something but she couldn't hear what it was. The sounds of the ocean outside had been amplified by some invisible technician working their eardrums. She asked him to repeat what he had said.

"I'd like to know if I'm going to be whipped...."

She had never thought of whipping anybody. She had outgrown the need to inflict pain on others for she was certain that pleasure was purposive in and of itself and that pain was a way of diverting attention from the transformative power of pleasurable experience. She would never whip or hit anybody. Unless they insisted that it was the only way they could actually experience or *accept* the concurrent experience of pleasure. She found this to be the case in many American men which is why she left them. But Mal was different and she knew he didn't want to be whipped. He was just letting her know that his complex need for her went beyond even what he himself felt was necessary.

"Do you know why I'm so fond of you?" she asked, looking down at him again, "or anyway *one* of the reasons I'm so fond of you? It is because you have always *accepted* me for what I am. You dig?"

"Hmm," Mal murmured and his stretched-out body shifted uneasily.

"And I know you love women," she went on, "oh boy, do you just love women or what?, and that you think of *me* that way—as a woman. Well, I do have all the qualities we usually

164

recognize as being feminine…." And whether through some alien intuitiveness, or whether she actually visualized it, she knelt down on the floor beside him and reached out gently resting her hand on his wet trousers cupping her palm over the taut wood-hard muscle beneath, raising her beautiful face to him with a smile that was lustrous and benign. "Is this for me?"

Mal opened his eyes and took in her radiance: "It's always been for you."

"Oh Mal, you're wonderful," she said with a marvelous laugh and slowly pulled down the zipper, took it out, holding it carefully, studying it. "Just look at it—all throbbing and eager, and no place to go."

"No place to *come*, you mean," said Mal trying to withstand the pressure of her obvious tease. She was the absolute best by far.

"Why does it have to be so huge?" she said, her head to one side regarding it with a studied look. "Maybe if it wasn't so big I could suck it."

"I'm sorry," said Mal.

"No, no, baby," she shrieked, "it's perfect. I wish *I* had one exactly like it. And look, it's *famished*," she touched a small glistening drop on its near-bursting blue head, "it's drooling." She sighed, and looked at him, now holding it firmly in her right hand. "It's gorgeous, isn't it Mal?" she admitted to herself and then threw her head back, dreadlocks falling behind her shoulders. "We must do something about it," she said and closed her eyes, moistened her lips and opened her mouth slowly, tenderly taking it inside her.

As she softly sucked him coating the thick member in her special brand of saliva, he reached over and slid his hand up over her chest firmly cupping her left breast, just holding it for a few seconds before tenderly taking the nipple between his thumb and forefinger. At the pressure, slight as it was, she almost imperceptibly recoiled—but then relaxed, yielding, even coming forward a little, as the nipple began to swell and distend while he softly squeezed and rolled it between his fingers. An urgent sensation took over her entire body as if Mal had worked the magic button and her response was to breath harder and grope with her hands searching for something more, finally finding and opening the top of his trousers, taking them down enough to grip her hands on his bare waist, and then his ass, quickly pulling him toward her, sucking voraciously, with gasps and moans, like a woman being made love to, almost painful—occasionally taking in so much that she gagged.

She looked up at him all breathless, glassy-eyed and shimmering with wet lips. "Are you going to come in Zulu's big, beautiful mouth?"

"Abso-lutely."

She nodded, closed her eyes, opened her mouth, then looked up at him, assuming her studied expression. "I guess I'll have to swallow all your delicious come too, won't I?"

"Yep."

She smiled her secret smile. "Good—because I want to swallow it—all of it."

She continued deepthroating his huge shaft and when he started to come, he let go of her breasts and took her head in his hands, holding it and pulling it to him, wanting to come inside the wonderful depths of her soft canal, to explode against the very back of her needing throat. And she devoured it, gulping and sucking as if in some insatiable desperation, until every drop was drained—and Mal, in a state of collapse, weakly pushed her head away.

166

"Wow," he murmured.

She looked up at him, her brown eyes flashing a galaxy of eros-transmission, happy in knowing she had taken in the core of his drugged crusade. "Hmm," her pink tongue moved around her glistening lips, "it's strange. There's so much of it and it's so *rich.*"

"Yes."

"It's tastes so...*alive.*"

"I'm totally smothered," said Mal and he curled up into a fetus position and slowly faded to sleep.

*

After they woke, Zulu said: "I'm beginning to question the relevance of my experience. For example, I see you and you see me. I experience you and you experience me. I watch you behave and you watch me behave. *We act certain ways to each other.* This acting is our experience of ourselves. Not ourselves *together*, because I can't experience your experience just like you can't experience mine, but ourselves as *individuals.*"

Mal was confused: "It sounds abstract. Besides, I feel like I live inside you. I'm just more you out here. You give birth to me over and over again."

"But, Mal, you have to accept certain realities: I do not experience your experience. Your experience of me. You say you feel like you live inside me, okay, that's what you feel, but I don't or can't experience that feeling. It's invisible to me. Only *you* can experience your experience of me. And me mine, of you. Or maybe not," she laughed and it sounded like the croak of death.

"Maybe not. But experience is relative to how we act toward each other and acting is always a false performance.

167

A made-up pretense. A fake-out. Cruel portrayal."

"Not always. I'm being me. I'm here, hearing you out, pursuing some magic connection that reinforces the truth of our experience."

"Yes, but you see, you just said OUR experience, so you *do* admit that it is something that can be transferred one to the other so that we *can* experience what the other experiences."

"I don't think so Mal, but you're brave for trying. It's why I dig you so much. You're not only a heat-seeking missile hitting designated target zones, you actually got soul."

"A soul is useless, though, I mean, souls suck. They're immortal. Black holes. That's where the body disconnects. It's like a spatial thing. One suddenly finds himself wandering the multi-layered depths of your jungle book, your algorhythmic zoo, nurturing himself inside it with all the other earth animals, hiding and living off its Nutrience until we die. And when we die, when our systems finally crash with no repair in sight, we get sent directly to your intestines, the trash heap of erroneous matter, where we curl up into a fœtal position becoming nothing but the decomposed matter of days gone by only to reemerge a short time later as your bowels whereupon you shit us back out into the soil. If you want to get in touch with this crazy cock's soul then check out the soil. Turn it. Mix it. Regenerate it. That's where you'll find the love, baby, it's nestled in the dirt. Nature's funny that way."

"Oh Mal, *you're* so funny that way. You are more of a *soul-*man than any of the other dicks I've ever had contact with. You're the only one who can make the Great Mother come."

"Well, the Great Mother sure made *me* come. I have *never...*"

"That's right, baby, and you never *will,* cuz the red earth cunt gobbles you better than wild turkey. If only you wouldn't run back to Amerika then maybe we could...but I know what you're thinking and I'm not going to stop you from finding out for yourself what I already know. You gotta do what you gotta do, baby, I'm just happy we carry these depths with us wherever we go."

Mal felt deeply connected to her. Their mouths found each other and became one long shadow kissing itself so intensely that they both ceased to breathe.

*

Mal standing on the golden sand staring at the mild ocean reflecting a wild full moon immediately realizes that he's leaving Lagos in a few hours. The sun will soon rise and this Therapeutic Recovery Zone will all end for him and he will go onto the next phase of his development (but is it really development or, rather, is it degradation, that is, just an illusion of growth that is inextricably tied to the amount of product he's capable of producing in one average lifetime?). He feels the impulse to move on but this impulse could be nothing more than a preprogramed disposition he has absolutely no control over. And he knows it. But why does he know it? He'd just as soon not know it and continue bumming on the beaches looking for fresh transient sluts. But there's no doubt in his mind what's happening: he really must be going.

He knows this to be true because his process of transition, of leaving one place and gradually entering another, is signaled by the fact that he starts dematerializing before he even actually departs the place he's been hanging in. This explains his inability to feel comfortable where he is right now, in front of the inviting sea and white menstruation fluid of the drippy moon in heat. Right now he knows he has to go back to his pad and pack his bag and that the early morning train will be pretty full and that he has to get a ticket early. As his body goes through the motions, his mind is already occupying a totally different virtual space. He is experiencing the space-time discontinuum.

The pad is quiet. No sign of the new lodger Lisa or the hopeless Tony. He leaves his key on the kitchen table with a short note saying he's gone and that the landlord will be by on Thursday and she can keep the place if she wants it. He packs his bag and goes to the portable computer where, before closing it up, he decides to open the Diary file whereupon he writes:

This feeling of being in transition often freaks him out but at the same time it also excites him. He calls it Melting Plastic Fantastic Time. Instead of feeling chained to the rhythm of corporate-sponsored multi-national work-time, he actively engages himself in a breakdown of superfluous identity and enters a flux that engenders new prototypes of consciousness geared toward the dismantling of conventional ego headtrips in hopes of facilitating heretofore unheard of radical subjectivities. These radical subjectivities, a multitude of possibilities residing in his heart, interpenetrate the realms of the Other. The realms of the Other are located in pockets of molecular desire where pleasure-junkies like himself open themselves up to the ultimate in high-tech body ejaculation.

He now knows his body to be the latest in state-of-the-art Warehouse design (built-in obsolescence?). The fiber-optic rewiring of his central nervous system is an attempt to synthesize the living word into a digital simulation of blood and sperm that once discharged flows into the most sensitive parts of the readymade body composing that of the Other. Once the readymade body of the Other has scanned for language viruses and has finally absorbed the digital simulation of eager spermatozoa restlessly seeking egg-unison, it then processes the new birth-trends of "meaning" that this nomadic connectivity has produced and immediately aligns itself with roaming pools of information that generate megabytes of molecular desire that form the forever metamorphosizing tribe of nomadic art terrorists.

The tribe of nomadic art terrorists is not made up of individuals with distinct characterizations composed of historical data informing segues toward Being. These conventional approximations of pseudo-identity only further disclose the artificiality of Being. Rather, the tribe de-defines clusters of unconscious spiritual energy by automatically unwriting so-called Being in fictional acts of flux-driven Becoming. TO DO OTHERWISE WOULD BE TO COMPLETELY ANNUL THE POTENTIAL OF FICTION AND ITS ABILITY TO RADICALLY DISSEMINATE THE BODY'S TRUTH.

*

Morning comes and the circle's complete. Still got no papamummy nature mind or god devil body or being life or nothingness. Nothing inside or out and above all no mouth to mouthe Being, that sewer drilled with teeth where man, who sucked his substance from me, looks at me all the time waiting to get hold of a papamummy and remake an existence free of me over and above my corpse taken from the void itself, and sniffed at from time to time.

I speak from above Time as if Time were not fried, which it is. Deep-fried and put in its Styrofoam coffin. This decomposed body fragment, expectorated from the anus of some immortal soul trapped inside this ludicrous notion of a human body and branded with the logo of a multi-national corporation, is a glob of fetal jelly rolled in petro-batter and flash-fried in a pan sizzling with rancid oil. Thrown in a box marked **CONSUME (IT'S GOOD FOR YOU!)** its gold marmalade eyes peer out in hopes of seeing it all stop and become anything but catastrophe. Too late. The "control variable" has peaked.

Picked up by lecher fingers stuck on greedy hands craving more greasy death in whatever form it comes. There's nothing left of me. I am completely burnt to a crisp.

"Uhmm," says the recently re-elected President, looking into the camera, telling it like it is: "these extra-crunchy alien moonbeams sure are finger-lickin' good."

Then cut back to his State of The Union message followed by complete analysis.

ESCHATOLOGY

Angels are dreaming of you...
Angels are dreaming of you...
Angels are dreaming of you...
Angels are dreaming of you...

—Sonic Youth

MANY YEARS LATER (AFTER HAVING ACHIEVED MODERATE SUCCESS AS A VOCALIST FOR AN ALTERNATIVE ROCK BAND CALLED **ACID PORN**):

"My body is giving up on me and my soul, what Tesla would call IMMORTAL:ONE®, seems ready to blow itself up in one final blast of verbal scatology. Shards of words disseminate haphazardly from deep inside my brain where the central control module, manipulated by some unknown force outside of me, attempts to reconstruct my ideological underpinning. Taking on a voice of its own, the central control module, connected to a Scanner Interface that constantly images pictures of myself doing things I used to manually do on my own, says to me:

'You are experiencing the consciousness of a fractal subject radically altered into a multitude of miniaturized egos (all similar to each other). This fractal subject constantly redoubles itself in an embryonic mode caught in a biosynthetic culture whose environment, a neuromuscular nonlinear mathematical model, gives birth to a schizogenesis of seemingly autonomic actions lost in The Myst. The Myst is a biological haze of uncertainty that grows inside a manmade body of over 80% nylon-water. It is said to be the result of a slow-death overdose of post-industrial waste. It attacks the immune system and causes the Scanning Interface one depends on for key visualization functions to occasionally fade to black. The blackout is totally disorienting. It makes the hairy automaton posing as a "human" worker feel powerless, as if something external has just pulled the plug on it.'

"The central control module's androgynous voice temporarily silences itself and my Scanner Interface is presently imaging a graphic display of my 'human' worker body as if it were some readymade rock star cranking out grunge chords in a flash-flood of anarchic video moments. These multi-media extravaganzas that take over my mind make me seem prehistorically savage as my body uncontrollably dances to the sounds of a digital climax warming in the feedback of a socially-distorted horizontal plane. Vague dreams of an erupting geophysiological four-dimensionality once again seem imminent as the imaging now shows my body on the edge of ejaculation. Just as I'm about to watch myself lose whatever polyphasic juice there might be left in me, the Scanner Interface starts crashing toward black, a warning signal advises me that there is a bus error, flashing the words **Matching Location Signatures Malfunction.** As I watch myself fade toward a darkness I have no control over, I realize I no longer have the power to see myself come. Apparently, that's for somebody else to experience, somebody who's either so rich or so brown-nosed that they're one of the few living beings capable of tapping into the power-connectivity of all the crucial networks that interpenetrate their copyrighted hyperspace. For Unidentified Frying Objects such as myself, this continued disenfranchisement from my own encoded life-forces is a way of proving to me over and over again that the Money-Cum-Power-Formula is everywhere.

"By the time my Scanning Interface starts coming back into focus the imaging is centered on two muscle-reflex models (they must be my own) that imitate a pair of 'human' muscles twitching in digital nervousness. The central control module inside my Scanner Interface cranks up the volume of the androgynous inner voice as it starts asking me random questions:

'All that wonderful sex for nothing? Where shall we go next? Terminate execution? Monitor progress? Being acquired? By who? Going where? "Execute termination." Why? Who said that? Is it too late to modify? One last time? Regenerate gender agenda? For what? To go where? For what? What's there? What IS it? What could it possibly be? Who are you now? Who am I now? Who are we now? WHAT are we? An optimal sequence achievement? Is this Truth or Dare? How has this happened? What advanced planning has led to its coordinated hierarchy? Who's responsible? Is this sequential system concurrent with Money-Cum-Power-Formulation? Is that a rhetorical question? Am I a double-headed shadow arrow inserting hidden messages into the routing tree or am I part of a heretofore unheard of rhizomatic writing and, as a last ditch effort, find myself appropriating the movement? Is it possible that the movement (WHAT movement?) has BECOME me and I'm just its point monitor? Wishful thinking? Why terminate execution? "Can I push your tender buttons?" What? Who said that? Can I push MY tender buttons? Why? For what purpose? To interact with the slutty software? Would pushing all the right buttons be just more preprogramed riffing I have absolutely no control over? Why work at it? Why work at all? Slave manipulation serves who? What kind of prototype are you anyway? You call this consciousness? For what purpose? Why deliver? Why deliver? Why deliver? What will having received these signals achieved for you? Negative affirmation? What is it that's being affirmed? Negative space? For what? What will have taken place inside it? Why continue? For who?'

"The androgynous voice stops its run-on questioning

once again and now there enters the image of a reconstructed version of Madonna who, having entered the Scanning Interface without prior notification, persists in slow-motion neuromuscular blowjobs fulfilling a series of skillful maneuvers that the unit's Analytic Record evaluates as 'superior in performance.' It feels good jerking my hyperreal narrative-load into her smooth steel throat lubricated with SOUL:2® unction so slick it makes me feel as though this graphic image of a jutting 'human' worker (is it really me?) is capable of spazzing inside her vacuum-powered cavity. My sequence achievement synchronizes with an optimum image scan of her peaking sexual simulation (stimulation?) so that all I can see are her skilled hips modulating temporary digital reflex in hopes of pulling in my IMMORTAL:ONE® *takeControl*® message. The Myst starts fuzzing in black patches so that it's almost impossible to focus on the near-ejaculation of my readymade polyphasic jism finally on the verge of coming again. Total black interference takes over again as central control module continues derailing me with unending questions:

'Is Tesla becoming a transvestite? Why does he wear a dress? Would this be an obstacle to our continued friendship? Is he the Controller? Can he manipulate Money-Cum-Power-Formulation? What makes him want to keep me alive? Is he initiating an entirely new sequential system that will redirect my image scans on those living-dead who have tons of hard information they desperately want to slip inside my all-too-open drive? Why did he say "terminate execution"? Is it he who wants to push my tender buttons? Is this some kind of character assassination? Who are these master-manipulators and why are they trying to meld me into the jesuschrist superstar MEISTER®

(Model Enhanced Intelligent and Skillful TEleoperational Rogue)? Why is this happening? Why can't we just stay in the isolated Screening Lab with its naked "human" worker bodies grooving on drugs, organic fruitjuices and loud grunge chords ripping our soft heads to shreds?'

"The voice falls to silence and I begin breaking through the black. I can actually feel myself desiring bodily ejaculation. I have to pretend like it's still possible. The spring-like interface between limb and environment makes me feel like the entire system that controls me is finally getting up enough nerve to turn off its amateurish Digital Climax Program and lift itself off the couch so as to walk to The Screening Lab for some much needed Nature Scene®. Ain't no high ever been seen like Nature Scene®. A strong dose and you're ready to create your own reel-time hyper-space. Instant Karma (virtual reality). More better orgasms (I constantly tell myself this is True. If I can convince myself then maybe I can convince the Others?). The Scanner Interface module acquires the images of me walking and asynchronously sends the images to the Image Queue Manager where I am let right in no questions asked. Once inside IQM I am already walking. I am walking inside myself scanning for other possible images. 'Human' worker bodies keep filtering in. So many hotsexy options at my disposal I almost feel the final implosion of Internal Oblivion herd me to my genealogical closure. And yet everything seems to move along perfectly as I enter The Screening Lab scanning for some of the high-potency blue-tinted Nature Scene® and upon seizure immediately ingest a small sheet causing the instantaneous rush of slick tendon-driven actuators tingling with 'human' excitement. This transmission of the antiquated 'human' feeling is so successful that I feel I have to transcribe it onto my PowerText® so I instinctively switch over to a synchronized control algorithm that models more word rain onto the color screen my face has become. The transcription is getting into Itself. My face is already flashing the improvisation of loaded messages:

ARGOT-4-3021
MOTOR COMMAND PATTERN IDENTIFICATION 7.2
FORCE-TIME PLOTS NARRATIVE-LOAD (DYSFUNC-TIONAL LUNACY DERIVES FROM "HUMAN" ELEMENT?)
EXPERIMENTAL DATA RECOVERY EMULATED POSITION
SIMULATED COMPLIANCE ::: CONSTRAINT MOTIONS
MUSCLE MODULATION : MALEDICTION MUZZLE
IMMORTAL:ONE? SOUL:2 (SLICK CUNT STEEL THROAT ALLOY COCK THROBBING BRAIN SATELLITE EXORBITANT COST: PROSTHETIC AESTHETICS)

Now that I'm high again and can feel the inner core of my spiritual hardness turn into a fatal erection full of high-tech killers and slaugh-tered victims bleeding empty images of daily life that mean nothing to me, something inside me stirs and I recognize it as the feeling of my bowels. It feels as though I could actually go to a toilet and take a shit again. What a thought. Not even 'human' workers can do *that* anymore. What a thought though: actually going to a shitter and letting part of myself go. What has happened to us? I *liked* going to the bathroom.

In this hypertextual state of elevated consciousness I immediately come to terms with the fact that my work, my trace, the mark of my thoughts that is nothing but the digital excrement that robs *me* of my possession after I have been stolen *from* my birth, must be rejected. I have sought to have a proper body and this is what kills me. Our need to become something other than our own shit denies us the opportunity to become spirit. Like all my brethren, my living flesh is opposed to everything that I am in the process of becoming. Birth, the initial theft that deprives me of myself, recycles this deprivation in quantitative mounds of pyramidal shit. Yet this stacked up monument of born-again waste is only a simulation of its former self. IT IS NOT THE REAL THING. I AM NOT THE REAL THING. I HAVE NOTHING LEFT TO WASTE. No time. No self. No work. No thoughts. No nothing. Why can't I stop myself from creating this huge shit-castle to get lost in?

ARGOT-4-3021
MOTOR COMMAND PATTERN IDENTIFICATION 7.2
IMPROVISATIONAL SEPARATION OF CONTROL PROCESSOR
FROM PURE BODY CONSTRUCT RECONSTITUTING VIGILANTE
VIRUS IN FORM OF SCATOLOGICAL HEARSAY
SHITTING GLUE OF MINDS STICKING TOGETHER

A modulated voiceover, apparently female genotype with phone-sex authority, explains to me that "the only thing that matters is the matter itself, the gaseous ripping-apart-at-the-seams, as if you were giving birth, as if oblivion were a gigantic shit waiting to happen, all thoughts finally executed in terminal grief, you, Mal, the cunning crapshooter who gambles with words that never come up when he wants them to, snake eyes (Maldoror), born loser, filling up with piles and piles of unexcretable shit, really full of shit now, more full of shit than you can ever remember being, rolling and staying awake at night unable to sleep because the shit demands your attention, it curls and curdles and cuddles up within you so that you never forget what you're made of, who made you (The Shit-God, the Ultimate Crap-ola), what you're worth (ain't worth a shit, that's for sure!), what your life has come to (the shit has hit the fan? you wish!), the fear embodying your trembling artist hand as it desperately tries to relate to this nominal irregularity (Mal-content), your odor, baby, the smell of unrealized decomposition (muy Mal)..."

ARGOT-4-3021
MOTOR COMMAND PATTERN IDENTIFICATION 7.2
LUNAR NODE SYNASTRY LODE MILKFLESH MODE
CYCLICAL CONJUNCTION INDICATING KARMIC
DHARMIC PATH TO OBLIVION STIMULATION
HARMONIOUS SEXTILE FLOW INTERFUNCTIONAL
PARTICIPATORY INTERPENETRATION OF
COLLECTIVE ACTUALIZATION {HEAVY LOAD}

Natural forces decompose all created matter so the

holding together of parts and artificial autonomy of a Modern Man is a lie. This text that delivers Itself to whoever can and wants to play with it tells Itself like it is. It isn't **like** anything. Not even Itself which is always in the process of becoming Something Else Altogether Different.

Itself is an animal who comes from the Mother. The Mother is a tongue loosely translating energy passing through the experience of writing which this is. I am the Mother Tongue.

Itself is a manipulated and controlled animal burrowing for a position. A position is hard to come by in contemporary Amerikan dick-penetrated society. Only by attaching Itself to a process of desire can Itself begin to write Itself out of the body. The body automatically unwriting Itself is what connects the process of desire to the soul-soil. The soul-soil turns in on Itself so as to connect with all the dirt that hangs out on the fringe of trademark Being. By marking Itself in the margins of a body processing the codes of a heretofore unwritten desire, Itself has become the alienation alienated from Itself.

Which is beautiful. Because an alienation so intense that it becomes alienated from Itself, is the purest form of existence a human has to offer Itself. As if one body could control Itself and be made up of many bodies (potential and actual). This extreme love of one's alienation is an act of terrorism. It disrupts the entire metaphysical cronyism of school, state, family, corporation. THEY CANNOT CONCEIVE OR CONSTRUCT ONE OF THEIR OWN. THEREFORE THEY PAY SOMEONE ELSE TO MAKE ONE FOR THEM. THIS IS THE

OPPOSITE OF SURVIVAL. IT IS GIVING IN TO DEATH. IT IS DEATH GIVING IN TO DEATH. IT IS THE GIVING OF DEATH (STEALING LIFE).

"The screen erases itself then reconfigures my face only after PowerText® depletes me of everything I could possibly own. My green eyes, the only organs I was able to keep, focus on the scene. Tesla is there with Madonna who is completely naked except for high-heels. Her butch haircut especially turns me on.

"'You know,' says Tesla, his wiry hair sizzling with bluish-green neon, 'there's a lot you don't know about me. For instance, on July 10, 1960, I was born-again in the town of Metlika, Slovenia. 50 years earlier, the *New York Times* had termed my life "spectacular." Now I am considered to be the Great Spectator who watches over the entire world. Micro-spectatorships engulf the globe and I am their Grand Wizard. Whatever life that is left on this decrepit planet depends on my secret vibrations in order to survive. Without these specially formulated currents of energy charging the inner regions of all our bodies, IMMORTAL:ONE® could not and would not exist. For this, the whole world owes me. But I never collect what I'm due because in an odd kind of way, I already *own* the world. It is also important for me to inform you that I have on many occasions condemned Woman as an anchor of the flesh who retards the development of Man and limits his accomplishments. This is a fact I was able to prove in the 18th century when I first started my experiments in Internal Oblivion. It was about two-hundred years later that I was offered the Nobel Prize. I refused to accept the Nobel Prize. No one before me or since has had the guts to do that. I don't need prizes, I don't need Women, I don't need patents, I don't need money-dope. I need vibrations. Energy. Electrical discharge.'

"'Oh baby,' says Madonna, instinctively embracing him in a bear hug that signals her affection for his toasted brain,

184

'I'm so *proud* of you. You have shunned the scientific world. You have shunned the world of emotions. You have shunned it all. I can love you just for *that*.'

"I'm too burnt from PowerText® to do or say anything. All I want to do is turn-on my flexible microactuator so as to shoot my SOUL:FLUID2® into her wares.

"'Yes,' Tesla keeps on, 'but you see, take Mal for example: He doesn't care about anything except orgasm. We have worked on him for centuries, and all he's capable of imagining is the rugged application of his material deformation onto your internal vibration. He knows only one thing: concurrency formulation. If he can somehow appropriate your on-going narrative-load then he'll be happy. All he cares about is his own happiness. Like most "human" workers lost in the lust of their need for somebody else's narrative-load, all he wants is to have a certain amount of control over his tip-direction. His conventional design is so makeshift it disgusts me. As long as he can maintain IMMORTAL:ONE® algorithms and continually regenerate SOUL:FLUID2®, he'll be as happy as a pig in slop.'

"'A what?' asks Madonna. She's new to the scene. Tesla had created her overnight.

"'Nevermind,' Tesla rambles, 'the important thing is to get you two totally in sync. If I can somehow get you two to inmix each other's internal vibration, without committing total oblivion, I'll have created the perfect superhuman energy current ever invented and then we can go DWB, Direct Wireless Broadcast, and infiltrate the homes and bodies of everyone! It'll be like a spiritual rebirth, a mass awakening, and I'll get to copyright myself as its Global Conductor! When I think of all those idiots copyrighting everything *but* that! What fools! Don't they know that The

185

Garden of Eden is a hotbox of perfectly mutilated electrical circuitry?! What fools!'

"'Oh Tess,' says Madonna as she squeezes his soft ass. 'What is it you wanna do with us?'

"Tesla answers her: 'Both of you will feel an intensification of internal pressure as the vibration I create for you over-stimulates your internal chambers. The pressure control valves will give way to the insistent pulse of this mysterious resonance I'll keep shooting you with. It'll feel like an orgone-drug is taking you over. At the point you become fully manipulated and are ready to discharge the SOUL:FLUID2® as if you were only *one* hypestar construct, I'll let you go live, Direct Broadcast. But you've got to be willing to give up part of yourself to become this crazy new thing I think will totally turn on the populace, particularly the youth.'

"'Uhmmm,' says Madonna, who, by now, is feeling up her silicone breasts with her fiber-reinforced rubber fingers. 'I wanna be It,' she continues, 'I wanna be free, different, ultra-rad, and I wanna come a lot, everywhere, all over the place, everybody.'

"Meanwhile, I'm just plain dead. I can't even see myself anymore. My narrative-load, though nonlinear and capable of creating a motor dynamic so virtual it could almost guarantee me the ultimate in reel-time integration, is rapidly becoming a part of her. I figure Tesla's sweet-talking is just a distraction until the internal vibe starts taking effect, which, all of a sudden, it does, causing me to spin in a sensual vertigo I can't help but lose myself in. I'm certain that this is it, that I'm finally ghostwriting my own story and that the neuro-muscular system that drives my alloy cock toward the heavens is no longer connected to my brain. My brain. The catastrophic trace of words turning into images turning into vibration. I feel myself becoming all vibration. A video flash of limbs and high-frequency vibrations. My whole system-construct becomes overexposed to the hot TV lights as the simulated walls of my supposed identity start crumbling. Borderless parameters melting. The last images I'm capable of registering get locked in my Scanner Interface. Stuck in a loop, the same set of images repeats itself over and over again, a close-up of my rubber pinchers reaching for Madonna's artificial breasts and as I touch them I can't feel them and so I tear them off and start shoving pieces into all my orifices and it feels like someone is raping me."